WETHERBY

also by David Hare

SLAG
TEETH 'N' SMILES
FANSHEN
A MAP OF THE WORLD
THE HISTORY PLAYS
Knuckle, Licking Hitler, Plenty

with Howard Brenton
BRASSNECK
(Methuen)
PRAVDA
(Methuen)

films for television
DREAMS OF LEAVING
SAIGON: YEAR OF THE CAT

WETHERBY

A FILM BY DAVID HARE

with photographs by
SOPHIE BAKER and NOBBY CLARK

faber and faber
LONDON · BOSTON
published in association with Greenpoint Films Ltd

First published in 1985
by Faber and Faber Limited
3 Queen Square London WC1N 3AU

Filmset by Wilmaset Birkenhead
Printed in Great Britain by
Whitstable Litho Limited
Whitstable Kent
All rights reserved

British Library Cataloguing in Publication Data

Hare, David
Wetherby
I. Title
822'.914   PR6058.A678
ISBN 0-571-13489-0

The photographs on pages 13 15 33 34 54 57
60 66 67 70 80 88 92
were taken by Sophie Baker and those on pages
11 14 17 20 22 26 31 38 40 49 51 61 68 71 73 76 78 84 86 90
by Nobby Clark

The première of *Wetherby*, a Greenpoint Film presented by Film Four International and Zenith Productions, took place at the Curzon West End, London, on 8 March 1985. The cast included:

VANESSA REDGRAVE as Jean Travers
JUDI DENCH as Marcia Pilborough
TIM MCINNERNY as John Morgan
IAN HOLM as Stanley Pilborough
STUART WILSON as Mike Langdon
SUZANNA HAMILTON as Karen Creasy

Other parts were played as follows:

The Wetherby characters

MARJORIE YATES	Verity Braithwaite
TOM WILKINSON	Roger Braithwaite
PENNY DOWNIE	Chrissie
BRENDA HALL	Landlady
MARJORIE SUDELL	Lilly
PATRICK BLACKWELL	Derek, Chrissie's husband

In the past

JOELY RICHARDSON	Young Jean Travers
ROBERT HINES	Jim Mortimer
KATY BEHEAN	Young Marcia
BERT KING	Mr Mortimer
PAULA TILBROOK	Mrs Mortimer
CHRISTOPHER FULFORD	Arthur
DAVID FOREMAN	Young Malay

The school

STEPHANIE NOBLETT	Suzie Bannerman
RICHARD MARRIS	Sir Thomas
JONATHAN LAZENBY	Boatman
NIGEL ROOKE	First page
JOHN ROBERT	Second page

7

NORMAN MILLS	Drama teacher
VANESSA ROSENTHAL	⎫
TREVOR LUNN	⎬ Pretentious parents
GUY NICHOLLS	Mr Varley
IAN BLEASDALE	Neurotic teacher
PETER MARTIN	Helpful parent
MOUTH, DAVE, DOB, FLASH, JONNY, LEBANON, TRACEY, BEZ, JEN, JESSICA, RHIANON, MADDY, PAUL, TOBY, MARCUS, MASHER, ANDY, JANET, PETER, RAM, LIZ, ED, SUZANNE, LESLEY, SHAUN	Miss Travers's class

The police

DIANE WHITLEY	Policewoman
MIKE KELLY	CID policeman
HOWARD CROSSLEY	Policeman
MATTHEW GUINNESS	Randall, the police doctor
TED BEYER	Police sergeant

Director	David Hare
Producer	Simon Relph
Associate Producer	Patsy Pollock
Music	Nick Bicât
Designer	Hayden Griffin
Director of photography	Stuart Harris
Costume designers	Jane Greenwood and Lindy Hemming
Editor	Chris Wimble

NOTE

The script as published does not correspond exactly to the final version of the film. In the editing I changed round a few scenes which I have here retained in an order which makes them easier to read.

D.H.

1. CREDITS.
Under the credits the sound of a conversation slowly drifts in, and then under it is established the sound of a crowded place. Their talk overlaps.

JEAN: (*Voice over*) Nixon? Yes.

STANLEY: (*Voice over*) Yes? You remember?

JEAN: (*Voice over*) Of course I remember.

STANLEY: (*Voice over*) It's funny how many people forget.

JEAN: (*Voice over*) Nobody forgets Nixon. And it wasn't so long ago.

STANLEY: (*Voice over*) Ten years.

JEAN: (*Voice over*) Already? My God.

STANLEY: (*Voice over*) What was happening in Wetherby ten years ago?
(*A silence.*)
He was a distinguished member of my own profession.

JEAN: (*Voice over*) What? Liar?

STANLEY: (*Voice over*) No, not liar. Solicitor. Well, lawyer. He trained as a lawyer.

JEAN: (*Voice over*) Liar or lawyer?

STANLEY: (*Voice over*) Is there a difference? I wonder, have you got time for another drink?

2. INT. PUB. DAY.
Continuation. There is a sudden silence, and the picture arrives. In intense close-up. We are looking at JEAN, *a thin woman with grey hair, in her late forties. A cigarette burns in front of her. Across from her is* STANLEY, *a rumpled, baggy, instantly likeable figure in a sports jacket with a check shirt and a tie. Through an archway at the back of the shot we can detect that we are in a pub. Light falls sideways, in great shafts, into the bar. But we are in the deserted restaurant.*

STANLEY: Wouldn't it be marvellous if Nixon walked in now?
Right now. You just can't help it, it would cheer everyone up.

9

(*He laughs. At the door of the pub a dog scampers in and is chased out.* FARMERS *stand drinking at the bar in wellington boots.*)

JEAN: Oh God, Stanley, you and I have lived in this town for too long.

(STANLEY *looks at her, then he looks down. There is a sudden seriousness in his manner.* JEAN *looks away, then he shrugs.*)

You know the best thing about Nixon, I'll tell you . . .

STANLEY: Shouldn't you be getting back to school?

JEAN: No, listen, I'll tell you. The one Nixon story, all right?

(*There is a call of 'Time, gentlemen, please' in the main bar, but* JEAN *is leaning forward, intent.*)

When he first met Pat, she didn't like him very much. So, after a bit, she said she didn't want to go out with him any more. 'Well,' he said, 'it breaks my heart, Pat, and I'll only stop dating you on one condition.' And she said, 'What's that?' 'That I can always be the chauffeur.' So when she went out with other men, to the cinema, say, Nixon would drive them. He'd drive them to the cinema, they'd get out, they'd go in, her and her date, and Nixon would *wait outside*. He'd wait outside during the whole film with a packet of popcorn or a piece of chewing-gum. Then out they'd come and he'd drive them home. Now. . . I ask you . . . what does that tell you about Nixon?

(STANLEY *smiles.*)

STANLEY: Jean . . . I ask you . . . what does it tell you about Pat?

3. EXT. JEAN'S HOUSE. NIGHT

A perfect Yorkshire farmhouse, rather dilapidated, set in the crook of a hill. Lights burning at its windows. Outside, a wild but tended garden. Old garden furniture, abandoned bicycles. An image of run-down serenity.

4. INT. JEAN'S HOUSE. NIGHT

Inside there is a dinner party going on at a big wooden table which is at the centre of the kitchen cum dining room which takes up most of the farmhouse's ground floor. Everyone at the table, save one person, is in their late forties or early fifties. They are all at their ease, with the dimmed lights, the emptied casserole dish, the green salad and cheese, the very many bottles of red and white wine.

JEAN: If you want to be loved in life, there's no use in having opinions.

VERITY: I think you're right.

JEAN: Who loves people who have opinions? The people who get loved are the people who are easy. Easy to get along with.

ROGER: Jean . . .

STANLEY: Have we lost the corkscrew? I can't do the bloody thing.

(STANLEY *is standing hopelessly trying to open another bottle of wine.* ROGER *and* VERITY *are looking at each other in the meaningful way of couples at dinner parties.* ROGER *is a*

*pedantic, meticulous man in his forties, in grey flannels and a
sports jacket.* VERITY *is a forthright woman, slightly
overdressed for the occasion, a natural member of the Geoffrey
Boycott supporters' club.* MARCIA *is a warm and funny woman
in her forties, naturally good-humoured and outgoing, a touch
insensitive. She has taken up Jean's point at the other end of the
table.*)

MARCIA: There's a new girl at work, at the library, the sort of
girl men fall for, vacant . . .

JEAN: Cool.

MARCIA: Distant, that's right. She doesn't really have a
personality, she just has a way of suggesting to men that
she'll be whatever they want her to be. Not a *person*, not a
real person . . .

(ROGER *smiles, easy, thinking he understands.*)

ROGER: What's she done, this girl?

MARCIA: Well, I'll tell you . . .

ROGER: Just *been* this thing you object to, or has she done
anything wrong yet?

MARCIA: She exists.

MORGAN: She's young.

(*This is the first time* MORGAN *has spoken. He sits, younger
and less drunk than the others. He is only 25, in corduroys. He
is heavy, self-contained, slow.*)

MARCIA: Yes, if you like. She's young. So . . .

MORGAN: It's an offence.

MARCIA: But there's no . . .

(*As she searches for the word, she becomes suddenly passionate.*)
her . . . nothing which is her. I look at the
young – truly – and I am mystified. Want nothing. Need
nothing. Have no ambitions. Get married, have children,
get a mortgage. A hundred thousand years of human
evolution, brontosaurus, tyrannosaurus, man. And the sum
ambition? Two-up two-down in the West Riding of
Yorkshire, on a custom-built estate of brick and glass.
(*Addressing the whole table, which is now stilled*) That isn't
right, is it? Can anyone tell me?

(ROGER *smiles, still cool.*)

ROGER: She's young. That's all you're saying. She's young.
   (*At once a large drop of water splashes on the table from the ceiling, right in front of him.* JEAN *giggles and looks up.*)
JEAN: Oh God.

5. INT. LANDING. NIGHT
MORGAN, *with a torch, coming down the stepladder that leads to the attic.* JEAN *is watching from the landing. The sound of the dinner going on in the distance.* MORGAN *stops on the ladder.*
MORGAN: I think it's fixed.
JEAN: Thank you.
   (MORGAN *is still a moment.*)
   A slate fell in the night. I was frightened to go up there.
MORGAN: It's all right.
   (*He stands quite still on the ladder.*)
   Shall we go down?

13

6. INT. CORRIDOR. NIGHT

JEAN *moving very quickly now along the darkened corridor that leads to the dining room from the bottom of the stairs.* MORGAN, *by contrast, comes much more slowly, dawdling slightly on the stairs.*

7. INT. LIVING ROOM. NIGHT

JEAN *comes out of the darkness and into the dinner party. She is now wearing grey flannel trousers. She walks past the chattering table and goes to get coffee from the stove.* MORGAN *slips back quietly to his place.* ROGER *looks across to where* JEAN *is now standing. He looks at her a moment, thoughtfully.*

8. INT. SCHOOL. DAY

A bright and cheerful nineteenth-century schoolroom. Wooden desks and chairs in deep brown. JEAN *standing, addressing a mixed-sex class, very attentive. They are all about 16.*

JEAN: Whether our faces show. This is the question.

(*Pauses. There is a moment for them to think about it.*)

We read a face. We look at a face, let's say, and into that face all sorts of things we claim to read. Mary here . . .

(*We look at a girl in the front row.*)

Or John . . .

(*We look at* JOHN. *Earnest, with ears that stick out and low eyebrows.*)

. . . whose face is sly. His face is sly. His features are sly. Is John a sly boy?

BOY: He's sly all right.

JOHN: I'm not a sly boy.

(*The children all laugh or smile.* JOHN *smiles too.*)

JEAN: Do we become the way we look? Or do we look the way we really are?

(*We look at* SUZIE BANNERMAN, *a girl sitting at the back.*
She is fresh-faced, very attractive and assured. She is 15. The
bell rings.)

Right, everyone, that's it. That was meant to be English.
(*The class begins to talk and leave. But we stay on* SUZIE. *She*
gets up and starts to walk down to JEAN *at the front.* JEAN *is*
murmuring to herself:) 'There's no art . . . to find the mind's
construction in the face . . .'

SUZIE: Miss Travers? I wondered . . . do you have time for a
chat?

9. INT. CLASSROOM. DAY

SUZIE *and* JEAN *are sitting opposite each other in the now deserted*
classroom. They are both at school desks.

SUZIE: Miss Travers, do you think there's any point in my
going on in the sixth form?

JEAN: Of course. Don't be silly. What makes you say that?

SUZIE: Well, it's just . . . whatever you do, you seem to end up
unemployed.

JEAN: Not everyone. But I do know what you mean.

SUZIE: You get a university degree, like in French, then what?
Maybe you get to be a secretary. And that's if you're lucky.
Honestly, I have really thought about it. I don't really think
it's worth it, you see.

JEAN: That's not what education is, though, Suzie. If you're
always thinking, I must *use* my education for a career, then
you're already thinking about education in the wrong way.
Education is a thing in itself, a way of fulfilling your
potential, of looking for ways of thinking, ways, which if
you're lucky, will help you not just in your career, but in
your whole life.

SUZIE: What ways?

JEAN: Well, ways of being ordered, I suppose. Having some
discipline in the way you think. Not always being
bull-headed, learning not to rush into things.

SUZIE: Do you think uneducated people do that?

JEAN: Well, I don't. No, not necessarily. I mean, sometimes.

SUZIE: Are they inferior for not knowing how to think?

16

JEAN: No, of course not.
   (JEAN *smiles, on the spot.* SUZIE's *questions have no side.*)
SUZIE: But if you have something . . . what you call a way of
   thinking, which they don't, surely you're saying you're
   superior?
JEAN: No, Suzie, of course I wouldn't say that.
SUZIE: What then?
JEAN: Different.
SUZIE: Better or worse?

10. EXT./INT. JEAN'S HOUSE. DAY
JEAN's *house from outside in the early evening sunshine.* JEAN *is
working, correcting exercise books. We hold the shot, as if seeing it
from someone's point of view. Now* JEAN *looks up from her work
and finds* MORGAN *standing there. She is at once tense. He is
holding a brace of pheasant.*

MORGAN: I brought you some pheasant.
>   (*She doesn't move. She just stares at him.*)
>   Am I disturbing you?
JEAN: No.
>   (*She takes the schoolbooks she is correcting and closes them, then puts them in a neat pile on the table. She lines her pencil up beside them. Then she gets up.*)
>   Come in. I'll make you some tea.
>   (*She goes into the kitchen.*)

11. INT. KITCHEN. DAY

JEAN goes across to the stove. She fills the kettle and puts it on the Aga. It is as if she is relieved to have something to do. He moves across to the table, and puts the pheasant down. Then he lifts the corner of the schoolbooks, as if to look inside the top one. There is a silence, as she looks out the window.

JEAN: I love the slow evenings, once the summer begins to come. It doesn't get dark until eight.
>   (MORGAN *watches her. She turns, smiling.*)
>   Are you staying with Marcia long?
MORGAN: No. I don't know Marcia.
JEAN: What? (*Looking amazed*) But you said . . .
MORGAN: What?
JEAN: When you came to dinner . . .
MORGAN: I met her on the doorstep.
JEAN: Who invited you?
MORGAN: No one.
>   (JEAN *almost begins to laugh.*)
JEAN: What are you . . . what . . . are you saying? I don't believe this. Are you saying . . . ?

12. INT. JEAN'S HOUSE. NIGHT

Flashback. We see from inside the house as the small group of people arrive together at the door. MARCIA *and* STANLEY *are greeting* JEAN. *Then* MARCIA *introduces* MORGAN *to* JEAN.

MORGAN: (*Voice over*) I met Marcia on the doorstep, I introduced myself.

13. INT. JEAN'S HOUSE. DAY
The present. JEAN *is looking at* MORGAN, *amazed.*
JEAN: I thought you came with *her.*
MORGAN: No.
    (*A pause.*)
JEAN: It's not possible.

14. INT. JEAN'S HOUSE. NIGHT
Flashback. We return to the scene as JEAN *reaches out her hand to greet* MORGAN. MARCIA *is already going on ahead into the house.*
STANLEY *is behind.*
MORGAN: (*Voice over*) Then I said 'John Morgan' and you shook my hand.
JEAN: (*Voice over*) Yes.
    (*We catch* JEAN's *response to the handshake.*)
    Ah, hello, hello. You brought an extra.
    (*But* MARCIA *has already gone on into the house, not hearing this.*)

15. INT. JEAN'S HOUSE. DAY
The present. MORGAN *and* JEAN *are now staring at each other.*
MORGAN *speaks quietly.*
MORGAN: And you accepted me.

16. INT. JEAN'S HOUSE. NIGHT
Flashback. JEAN *moves round the warm, candlelit table, laying some knives and forks by the already set places.* ROGER *and* VERITY *are in nearby armchairs.*
JEAN: I'll lay an extra place.
    (*She looks across.* MORGAN *smiles.*)
MORGAN: Thank you.

17. INT. JEAN'S HOUSE. DAY
The present. JEAN *is staring at him, a more serious worry now in her voice.*
JEAN: Absurd! It's impossible!
MORGAN: No.
    (*He looks at her a moment, then takes a revolver out of his*

19

pocket and puts the end of it in his mouth. He blows his brains
out. His skull explodes across the room.)

18. EXT. JEAN'S HOUSE. DAY
Briefly, Jean's house seen from outside. The sound of a great cry
from inside.
JEAN: (*Out of vision*) No! No!

19. INT. AIRPLANE. NIGHT
At once flashback to 1953. We are inside a troop carrier. Rugs are
laid out on the floor. The airplane is darkened, silent, but for the two
people making love, naked on the floor. The YOUNG JEAN
TRAVERS *is stretched out, her head against the metal.* JIM *is 22,*
passionate. They are both sweating. We watch them, close in.
YOUNG JEAN: Yes! Yes!
JIM: No! Don't let me . . . no!
YOUNG JEAN: Yes!
JIM: No!
YOUNG JEAN: No, you mean, yes . . .
JIM: I mean yes. Yes!

20. EXT. AIRFIELD. NIGHT
Flashback, 1953. The darkened airfield. A wide flat space. The
windsock billowing in the night. Beyond, the great hangar. The
moon.

21. INT. AIRPLANE. NIGHT
Flashback, 1953. In the plane, they are now lying in each other's
arms. A rug covers them.
YOUNG JEAN: Let me see . . . let me look at you.
   (*She lifts the rug to look at his naked body. Then she lifts her*
   head and looks him full in the face.)

22. INT. AIRPLANE. NIGHT
Later. YOUNG JEAN *is sitting along the side of the plane. She has a*
blanket wrapped round her. She is on the benches where the troops sit
to be flown out. She has a pack of cigarettes and a lighter. She lights
a cigarette.

JIM: You're not meant to.

YOUNG JEAN: I know.

> (*In the cockpit* JIM *sits naked in the pilot's seat.*)
> Do you fly these?

JIM: Not a chance. Engine fitters don't get to fly. It's three years before you get to go on a flying course. Longer, maybe. And then not one of these.

YOUNG JEAN: Really?

JIM: They take the troops out in these. To the jungle.

YOUNG JEAN: Ah.

JIM: To the war. You come down seven times before you get to Malaya. It takes over a week. By the time you get there, you know you've been travelling.

YOUNG JEAN: I'm sure. (*A pause.*) Did you know . . . did you realize you might have to fight when you joined?

JIM: You're an airman, you want to fly. You're a soldier, you
    want to fight. Not much point else.
YOUNG JEAN: No.
JIM: I'll walk you home.

23. EXT. AIRFIELD. NIGHT

Flashback, 1953. JIM *shooting the bolt on the outside of the door.
He shoots another. Then a padlock, which clicks. He turns and
smiles at* YOUNG JEAN *who is standing nervously on one side. They
are dwarfed by the enormous tin wall of the hangar. They begin to
walk along the tarmac path. As they pass the mess, we see in the
steamed-up windows to a brightly lit room full of airmen, drinking
and singing. As they are about to pass, the door bursts open, and
crashing through comes an* AIRMAN, *who falls to the ground,
followed by others, all holding pints.*
AIRMEN: Make him drink it! Make him drink it!
    (*The* AIRMAN *on the ground protests. Instinctively* JIM *reaches
    for* JEAN, *touching her arm, covering her.*)
YOUNG JEAN: It's all right.
    (*They pass on. The* AIRMEN *become distant figures, forcing
    drink down the man's throat as he lies on the ground. Noises of
    protest and excitement, tiny figures in the vast night.*)

24. EXT. VILLAGE. NIGHT

Later. JIM *and* YOUNG JEAN *walk through the village, which has a
thirties feel to it – redbrick, suburban. Lampposts. A car or two.*
JIM: Happen if I were killed, I'd still say, fine. I joined to fight.
    Didn't have to. Could just have done National Service,
    tramped the parade ground. And we're not even at war.
    Well, not properly at war. Half a war. Malaya's half a war.
    (*Smiles.*) But I liked the idea.
    (*They stop by Jean's house. A semi in the style of all the others.
    A light is on upstairs.*)
    Is your mum in bed?
YOUNG JEAN: I think so. (*Puts a hand on his chest, flat, just
    touching the material.*) If she ever asks, we saw *The Third
    Man.*

25. INT. HOUSE. NIGHT

Flashback, 1953. YOUNG JEAN *standing at the bottom of the stairs, looking up, listening. Then she goes into the small fifties kitchen. There is a larder, she reaches for a piece of cheese wrapped in greaseproof paper. She goes upstairs. On the landing she pauses, as she goes to the door of her room. She calls to her* MOTHER, *unseen, in the other bedroom.*

YOUNG JEAN: Still awake?

JEAN'S MOTHER: (*From her bedroom*) Yes. How was it?

YOUNG JEAN: Good.

26. INT. JEAN'S ROOM. NIGHT

YOUNG JEAN *turns on the light in her room. It is the plainest lower-middle-class bedroom. Simple desk, bed, chair. The desk is covered with books and papers. It is clear she is studying for an exam. She looks ruefully at the empty room. Then she calls:*

YOUNG JEAN: Orson Welles killed all these children, but then they shot him in a sewer in the end.
　　(*A pause.*)

JEAN'S MOTHER: (*From her bedroom*) That's good.

YOUNG JEAN: Yes. Good night.

27. INT. JEAN'S ROOM. NIGHT

A little later. We look at the top of the desk. The piece of cheese is sweating in its greaseproof paper. The surface of the desk is covered with exercise books. YOUNG JEAN's *hand as she pushes a couple of books aside. Underneath, a black diary with a clasp, which she opens. Good, neat handwriting. She takes a pen, about to make an entry.*

YOUNG JEAN: Never dreamt, never thought any such happiness possible. Hiding in the dark, loving a man in the dark.
　　(*Although she is very quiet, she now makes a small eye movement in the direction of her mother's room. Her pen is poised.*)
　　Never knew any such happiness possible at all.

28. EXT. LANE. EVENING
The present. A single police car travelling along a country lane. Like a mirage, silent, serene.

29. EXT. JEAN'S HOUSE. EVENING
The police car coming up the short drive to the house. Outside there are three or four other police cars and an ambulance. The car gets near and stops. MIKE LANGDON *gets out. He is almost 40, with a moustache. He is in plain clothes. He looks towards the door where a* WORKMAN *is taking a lock off the door and putting a new one on. As* LANGDON *moves towards the door he pauses a moment, taking in his breath. As he does, he catches the eye of a young* POLICEWOMAN, *a sharp-featured blonde girl of about 23.*
LANGDON: How bad is it?
　(*The* POLICEWOMAN *doesn't reply.*)

30. INT. JEAN'S HOUSE. EVENING
LANGDON *comes into the room where four or five people are working in silence, clearing up all the furniture which has had to be moved.* MORGAN'S *body is still there. A* POLICE DOCTOR *is examining it. A* POLICEMAN *in uniform unwraps a piece of lint and shows* LANGDON *the gun.* LANGDON *nods. Then the* POLICEMAN *takes it away and almost at once from the other side another* POLICEMAN *holds up a plain snap of John Morgan. It is the simplest student mugshot.*
LANGDON: Why did he do it?
POLICEMAN: Depressed, I suppose.
LANGDON: Why did he do it in here?

31. INT. JEAN'S HOUSE. EVENING
The room much quieter now. Only the sharp-featured POLICEWOMAN *stands where Jean stood earlier. A* YOUNG POLICEMAN *sits where Morgan once was. By the wall, a group of* UNIFORMED POLICEMEN *and a* POLICE PHOTOGRAPHER, *watching with* LANGDON. *The* POLICEWOMAN *stares out the window.*
POLICEWOMAN: 'I love the warm evenings.' Something. Tea.
　(*Reaches for the teapot.*) 'It doesn't get dark until eight.'

(*Turns and faces the* YOUNG POLICEMAN.) 'How long are you staying with Marcia?'

YOUNG POLICEMAN: 'I'm not.'

POLICEWOMAN: Shock. Move towards him. (*She does.*) 'What d'you mean?'

YOUNG POLICEMAN: He explains.

POLICEWOMAN: 'Unbelievable!'

(*The* YOUNG POLICEMAN *reaches into his right pocket.*)

YOUNG POLICEMAN: Right pocket.

(*He mimes getting a gun out. He then sticks the two fingers of his hand into his mouth.* MIKE LANGDON *watching this. Then the* YOUNG POLICEMAN *and the* POLICEWOMAN *both look to the floor.*)

That's it.

32. EXT. GARDEN. NIGHT

MIKE LANGDON *sits alone now in the deserted garden of Jean's house. He is stretched out in a chair, looking to the house. He is thinking. Then he gets up and goes back in.*

33. INT. JEAN'S HOUSE. NIGHT

LANGDON *walks along the side of the kitchen, running his hand along the surface, thinking. The neat range of objects: the herbs, the olive oil, the garlic. The cookbook open at 'Coq au vin'. Still thinking, he moves towards the other part of the room. On the mantelpiece, an invitation to a local amateur dramatic society. A school photo of Jean's class. A photo of the house. A couple of candlesticks. A photo of Jean as a young girl, standing beside the young Marcia. He reaches towards it.*

JEAN: There seems little point . . .

> (LANGDON *reacts sharply, as in guilt.* JEAN *has come into the room from the hallway and is standing in the door. She looks gaunt.*)

LANGDON: My goodness, I'm sorry, you startled me.

> (JEAN *nods at the new lock on the door, where it is gleaming conspicuously. She goes over to it.*)

JEAN: The new lock. The chances of the same thing happening twice. (*Turns and looks at him.*) And anyway I let him in.

> (LANGDON *looks across the room at her.*)

Doesn't matter how well locked up you are, at times you're always going to have to let people in.

> (*She looks at him a moment, then crosses the room and stoops down below him to switch on the electric fire.*)

LANGDON: Are you all right?

JEAN: Yes. I've been trying to sleep. As best I may.

> (JEAN *stops involuntarily, seeing something we do not see.*)

LANGDON: Oh yes, I'm sorry. We don't clean up afterwards. We just take the body away. It seems a bit callous, I know. But the thinking is if we always had to clear up, the police would spend their whole life on their knees.

> (*Pause.*)

JEAN: How are you getting on?

LANGDON: Well, we have something.

(*He moves away, the photo of Jean and Marcia still in his hand.*)

He was a student.

JEAN: I see.

LANGDON: Working for his doctorate at the University of Essex. He came to the town a few days ago and rented a room.

JEAN: Are you a graduate yourself?

LANGDON: Yes. A subject of much mirth. A graduate policeman. (*Smiles, waiting to see what her reaction will be.*) This man wasn't my generation. He was younger, he was only 25. He came to research at the British Library down the road.

(JEAN *has sat down.* LANGDON *looks at her a moment.*)

A blankness. A central disfiguring blankness. That's what people who knew him describe.

(JEAN *nods slightly.*)

JEAN: Yes . . . it's true . . . I've been trying to remember. At dinner he said so little. Until late in the evening. He seemed already set on a path. (*Smiles.*) It's funny, I mean, looking back, I took his being there for granted. Even now it doesn't seem odd.

LANGDON: Well, that's right, I've often been out to dinner, and not been quite sure who somebody was.

JEAN: No.

LANGDON: Quite.

(*There's a pause.*)

Though usually it's different if you're the hostess.

(*He waits for the reaction. But she says nothing.*)

Anyway, it turns out it wasn't completely out of the blue. The day before he'd seen Marcia Pilborough. As you know, she works at the library . . .

JEAN: Oh, I see.

LANGDON: . . . and he'd gone up to her, they'd had a conversation. He wanted to borrow a book. Afterwards we think he probably waited and started to follow her.

JEAN: Ah, well. Yes. It begins to make sense.

(LANGDON *looks at her a little nervously.*)

LANGDON: Would you say . . . I mean these things are very

difficult . . . would you say that Marcia was in any way a
woman who was likely to have been deliberately
provocative? I mean, is lying and brought him to dinner
deliberately? Or as a joke?

(*For the first time* JEAN *smiles very slightly.*)

JEAN: I don't want to be rude about Marcia – she's my best
friend – but I'm afraid I don't think that possible at all.

34. EXT. RIVERSIDE. DAY

*At once flashback (1953) to the sound of two girls as they walk
together along a riverside, densely vegetated, the river running silver
in the sun beside them.* YOUNG MARCIA *is plump, likeable,
unpretentious. Her hair is permed.* YOUNG JEAN *walks beside her
with a garland of daisies in her hand.*

YOUNG JEAN: And London, tell me, what would that be like?

YOUNG MARCIA: London? Oh, wonderful, London would be
wonderful. Just totally different. Not like Wetherby in any
way.

(JEAN *puts the garland on* MARCIA's *head.* MARCIA *laughs.
They embrace.*)

YOUNG JEAN: Hold on, look, you look lovely.

YOUNG MARCIA: Really?

YOUNG JEAN: Yes.

YOUNG MARCIA: I can't go back into town like this.

YOUNG JEAN: Why not?

(*They smile and carry on walking.*)

YOUNG MARCIA: It's so exciting, the idea of living in a great
city. People say, oh, cities are so anonymous. But that's
what's so good about them. Nobody knows who you are.

(JEAN *takes a sideways glance at her.*)

YOUNG JEAN: Marcia . . .

YOUNG MARCIA: Don't you long to get out?

YOUNG JEAN: Marcia, I'm . . .

YOUNG MARCIA: What?

YOUNG JEAN: I'm seeing an airman.

YOUNG MARCIA: Cripes! Are you serious? Does your mum
know?

(JEAN *looks down.*)

29

I'm seeing a soldier.
(*They burst out laughing.*)
Well, what on earth are we all meant to do?

35. INT. JEAN'S HOUSE. NIGHT

Flashback. The dinner party. The two women, MARCIA *and* JEAN, *are embracing by the stove – thirty years on from the previous scene. Behind them, people are talking.* JEAN *has a glossy photo in her hand.*

JEAN: Oh, Marcia, thank you.

MARCIA: I knew you'd like it.

JEAN: When did you take it?

(*She holds it up. A picture of the house. Still, unchanging, beautiful.*)

My house.

(*She moves across to the table where the guests are beginning to sit down.* STANLEY *is in the middle of the room, looking round.*)

Look, everyone, what Marcia's brought me. A picture of the house. Do you like it?

(*For the first time in this sequence we see* MORGAN. *He is now sitting at the edge of the room, all by himself.*)

MORGAN: It's great.

(JEAN *looks at him a moment, struck by his tone.*)

36. INT. JEAN'S ROOM. NIGHT

Flashback, 1953. The YOUNG JEAN *making love to* JIM. *He is pressing her against the wall. She has her legs up around him. She is laughing. A single light is on at the desk, her books and papers lit.*

YOUNG JEAN: Jim, no, don't, for goodness' sake . . .

(*He presses further into her.*)

Goodness . . .

(*She laughs.*)

JIM: Is this a party wall?

(*He presses twice more. Peals of laughter. She takes his head into her hands.*)

YOUNG JEAN: Jim.

JIM: What?

YOUNG JEAN: Please, it's undignified.

JIM: Unladylike.

> (*They smile. Very fond of each other.*)

YOUNG JEAN: Yes.

> (*The sound of a door opening downstairs. A key in the latch, the front door opening.*)

Jim, oh Lord, it's my mother.

JIM: What?

YOUNG JEAN: Let me down.

> (*He looks at her, presses her harder against the wall, holding her there, with his hands pressed against the wall.*)

JIM: (*Quietly*) I want to make love to you.

YOUNG JEAN: Jim . . .

> (*We are in very close. First on* JEAN, *then on* JIM, *as they look at each other without moving. There is a long stillness. Then the sound of lights being turned on downstairs. Then off. A creak*

on the stairs. Then movement, we stay on their faces. JEAN'S
MOTHER *calls from outside.*)

JEAN'S MOTHER: Jean, are you home?

YOUNG JEAN: I'm home.

JEAN'S MOTHER: Is there anything you need?

YOUNG JEAN: No, no, I'm fine.

(*There is a silence, then the sound of another door opening and a
light switch. The door closes.* JIM's *face as he looks at* JEAN,
both way above the situation, heightened, in love. JEAN's *face.
A slow cross-fade to:*)

37. INT. KITCHEN. NIGHT

*The present. Moonlight falling through the window on to a totally
cleaned-up, unreally tidy kitchen. The pair of pheasant lie in the
foreground, rotting slightly. The photo of the house, now on the
mantelpiece. Moonlight falling across it. A slow cross-fade to:*

38. INT. BATHROOM. NIGHT

JEAN *lying in the bath. She is stretched out, naked. There is a slight
ripple as she reaches for the ashtray beside the bath, to knock the ash
off the end of the cigarette. Then she takes a drag.*

39. INT. TRAIN. DAY

*Flashback. The central aisle of a British Rail train careering fast
through the countryside. It is full. Down the central aisle, a brown
holdall on his back, comes* MORGAN, *in a green anorak. He walks
on down. He is looking for a seat. And yet he looks neither to one
side nor the other.*

40. EXT. STATION. DAY

*Flashback. A small country station, just two platforms on either side
of the rails. The train rushes through at enormous speed. It is briefly
shaken by the passage, then is still. The danger has passed.*

41. INT. BOARDING HOUSE. DAY

*Flashback. Coming up the darkened stairs of a small boarding
house, a* LANDLADY *is leading* MORGAN. *Then they come to a
landing and she opens the door. The room is florally decorated,*

with wallpaper of roses and a quilt with creepers and flowers on it.
He goes in. She stands outside. MORGAN looks at the cosy but
desolate little room.

LANDLADY: Do you know how long you'll be staying?

MORGAN: (Closing the door) Oh . . . just a couple of days.

    (The LANDLADY goes. MORGAN lifts his holdall on to the bed.
He unzips it. He takes out a pair of pyjamas which he puts on
the bed. Then he sets a pile of books on the dressing table. He
puts down a fat file, his thesis. We see the title: 'The Norman
Village in the Thirteenth Century'. Then he reaches into the
bottom of his holdall and takes out a gun. He goes to the
window. It is covered by a thin pair of floral curtains. He
draws one back. The window overlooks the town square in
Wetherby. People are walking about, shopping, going about
their work. They are predominantly middle-aged. MORGAN

33

looks down on them, the gun in his hand, the sniper thinking
about possible targets. Some schoolchildren go by, an older
woman.)

42. EXT./INT. SQUARE. DAY
Flashback. From the square we look up to the first-floor window.
MORGAN *standing at the window, the gun not visible, dark, to one*
side. The sniper in place.

43. INT. JEAN'S HOUSE. DAY
The present. MARCIA *is sitting quite still by herself in the kitchen.*
Then STANLEY *arrives with groceries in a brown paper bag and she*
gets up to greet him and take them from him.
MARCIA: Ah, well done, Stanley. Thank you.
　　(She goes and puts them down on the kitchen slab.)
　　(Calling upstairs) Jean, we've got you some breakfast.
JEAN: *(Out of vision)* Thank you, Marcia. I'm just coming down.
　　*(*MARCIA *nods at* STANLEY *who is holding the morning paper*
　　which he has picked up from the doormat.)

34

MARCIA: Take the paper, Stanley, hide it. (*Calling upstairs again*) We brought you bacon and eggs.

(*We glimpse the headline, 'Mystery Suicide at Wetherby Woman's House'.*)

STANLEY: Why hide it? After all, she was there when it happened.

MARCIA: Stanley, she doesn't want to be reminded. Would you?

(JEAN *has appeared from upstairs. She is standing in the doorway. She is gaunt, sobered, changed.* MARCIA *turns from the stove.*)

Good morning. No paper, I'm afraid. I think there's a strike.

(*She turns to cook.* STANLEY, *who is half-heartedly holding the paper behind his back, turns to* JEAN *with a look of 'What can you do?'* JEAN *goes to get a glass of water.*)

STANLEY: All right?

JEAN: Well, I'm not in the pink.

MARCIA: I shouldn't wonder.

STANLEY: Did you sleep?

JEAN: I had dreams.

(MARCIA *has begun to fry bacon.*)

MARCIA: Does anyone know why he did it? And why on earth did he choose to come and do it to you? It was me he met first. I don't know why I didn't *think* at the dinner. I'd already met him. He could have done it to me.

(JEAN *sits at the table, where the party was.*)

JEAN: I think the lonely recognize the lonely.

MARCIA: You're not lonely.

(JEAN *looks a moment to* STANLEY. MARCIA *shoves away the cat which has been attracted by the smell of bacon.* JEAN *looks away.*)

JEAN: I only want coffee.

MARCIA: Stanley, d'you mind? Go and do something useful. Do you know how to do it with a filter?

(*She nods at the coffee grinder.* STANLEY *goes to work it.* MARCIA *turns again from the frying pan.*)

Have you searched back? Over all your behaviour? You know, did you offend him in some way? That's what I've

35

been thinking. Perhaps we upset him. Perhaps you looked like his mother, now that is possible. I read in a book . . .
(JEAN *interrupts, her voice clear and simple.*)
JEAN: I think it was more what we shared.
MARCIA: What's that?
JEAN: I told you. A feeling for solitude.
(*There is a pause.* MARCIA *is not convinced by this. She turns the bacon quite vigorously.*)
MARCIA: Well, you may have felt that. But to shoot your head off . . .
(JEAN *puts her hand to her mouth, interrupting her, this time urgently.*)
JEAN: Please, the bacon's too much.
MARCIA: Oh God, I'm sorry, it never occurred to me. I didn't think, oh Lord . . .
(*She turns, panicking, the pan in her hand, not knowing what to do with it.* STANLEY *goes to open the door.*)
STANLEY: Take it out.
MARCIA: Honestly, I'm sorry, Jean. It's out, it's almost gone . . .
(STANLEY *stands at the door.* MARCIA *has gone. Through the window she is seen to be holding the frying pan under the garden hose which is attached to an outside tap.* STANLEY *and* JEAN *look at each other meanwhile. Then he speaks very quietly.*)
STANLEY: If you're frightened of loneliness, never get married.
JEAN: I'm not frightened. (*Begins to cry.*) I'm hardened by now.

44. INT. THE MORTIMERS' HOUSE. DAY
Flashback, 1953. The YOUNG JEAN *is being led through the hall to the front room of the Mortimers' house. She is wearing a green floral dress and looks very fresh and clean.* JIM *is beckoning her in, to where his* MOTHER *is waiting in the front room. A small, eager woman of nearly 50. There is a fire burning and tea is set out on the table.*
MRS MORTIMER: Come in, come in.
(MR MORTIMER, *an equally small man in a suit, dressed for the occasion, gets up. The room could not be simpler. There is a fire burning in the grate.*)

MR MORTIMER: Ah.

MRS MORTIMER: Nice to meet you.

JIM: This is Jean.

YOUNG JEAN: Mrs Mortimer.

> (*They shake hands.*)

MRS MORTIMER: And this is Jim's father.

YOUNG JEAN: Hello.

MRS MORTIMER: Please sit down.

YOUNG JEAN: Gosh, look . . .

MRS MORTIMER: I baked you some scones. And there's Battenburg cake.

> (JEAN *smiles.*)

MR MORTIMER: You're looking very thin, lad.

JIM: Nay, I've been fine.

45. INT. THE MORTIMERS' HOUSE. DAY

Later. They all have teacups and the remains of scones on their knees.

MR MORTIMER: And so you'd be giving up college?

YOUNG JEAN: No, I don't think so, Mr Mortimer.

MR MORTIMER: Ah.

YOUNG JEAN: Jim thought as he'd be away for so long and so often, it's better if I occupy myself. I think I have a place at the University of Hull.

MR MORTIMER: Are you sure?

> (*He turns to* JIM, *who says nothing.*)

I don't think a woman who's going to get married should be thinking of going off away from her home.

YOUNG JEAN: But Jim won't be there. He'll be in Malaya.

MR MORTIMER: Ay, but he'd want to know that you're where you belong.

YOUNG JEAN: What difference can it make if he'd not be with me?

MR MORTIMER: He'll want to know you're at home.

> (JEAN *looks a moment to* JIM *for confirmation to go ahead, for the conversation which has started out easily is becoming a little tense.*)

YOUNG JEAN: I can't see honestly it'll make any difference. Any

home life we have is bound to be interrupted. At least from
the start. We'll see each other so little for a bit.

MR MORTIMER: Seven years, is that right?

YOUNG JEAN: Well, not necessarily . . .

(*She is about to go on.*)

MR MORTIMER: Doesn't Jim speak?

(*There is a pause. They all look to* JIM, *who is quiet.*)

JIM: The Air Force'll give me a house later. When I'm back
from active service. For now it's nice if Jean goes on with
her books.

(*There is an awkward silence. To break it,* MRS MORTIMER
holds a plate out.)

MRS MORTIMER: More Battenburg?

YOUNG JEAN: Did you bake it yourself?

MR MORTIMER: Don't be daft.

46. EXT. STREET. EVENING

Flashback, 1953. JIM *and* YOUNG JEAN *walking together along the
deserted Oldham street. It is evening. There is nobody about and the
light is about to go. Terraced redbrick houses on either side.*

JIM: You shouldn't worry.

YOUNG JEAN: They made me feel stupid.

JIM: Why?

YOUNG JEAN: Perhaps it is silly. Impractical. We've never really
met, you and me. We're always so happy together. It never
occurs to us that there's a world of people out there. We
can't spend our life . . .

JIM: What?

YOUNG JEAN: Just . . . with the sheets up over our heads.

(*The whole street is now seen, bathed in exquisite light.*)

JIM: How could you make Battenburg? No one can *make*
Battenburg. Half of it's pink.

YOUNG JEAN: Jim, I know. I was frightened. That's all.

(*They turn a corner. More streets, also deserted. A last bus.*)

JIM: Last bus.

YOUNG JEAN: Already?

JIM: You know nothing. This is a pig of a town.

47. INT. POLICE STATION. DAY

The present. A desk on which a row of photos have been laid out. Above, an Anglepoise lamp is the only source of light. The photos form a sequence: Morgan sitting at the table with his head blown off, in full-length shot, but each successive shot seeing him from a different angle. Then photos of the gun, and fingerprints. RANDALL, *the police doctor, showing them to* LANGDON.

RANDALL: The angle . . .

LANGDON: Yes.

RANDALL: . . . of the body means that murder is probably
　　　discounted. (*Points along the row to the close-ups of the gun.*)
　　　Forensic evidence, fingerprints. Nobody else has touched
　　　the gun. At the inquest I shall be arguing it's suicide.
　　　(LANGDON *opens the curtains. We see outside his small,
　　　modern office to green fields stretching away.*)
　　　You look disappointed.

LANGDON: No. Not at all.

48. EXT. JEAN'S HOUSE. NIGHT

LANGDON *stands in the garden looking up to the lit window of Jean's house. Then he moves away to his car.*

49. INT. POLICE STATION. DAY

Langdon's office now revealed in daylight. LANGDON *is adjusting a black tie which he is putting on in the mirror. The* POLICEWOMAN *is watching him.*

POLICEWOMAN: Where is it?

LANGDON: Derby. That's where he came from.

> (*A* POLICE SERGEANT, *uniformed, comes into his office, carrying a couple of chairs. He's followed by two other* UNIFORMED MEN, *carrying more chairs.*)

SERGEANT: All right if we come in here, Mike? The lads need some space. New fire-hose demonstration.

LANGDON: Not in here, for Christ's sake.

SERGEANT: Not real hoses, you idiot. Slide show.

> (*They are setting chairs down around the desk where the photos of Morgan are still laid out.* LANGDON *looks across, unsure whether to object.*)

No problem, Mike? All right? Put your thumb up your bum for a bit?

> (LANGDON *turns and goes out of the room, into the main part of the police station, where a group of* UNIFORMED MEN *are sitting laughing at a pornographic magazine. As he leaves, we just catch:*)

> (*To a* UNIFORMED MAN) CID do fuck-all anyway.

> (*But* LANGDON *is already being called over to the group sitting on the edge of the desk.*)

FIRST POLICEMAN: Hey, Mike, look at this.

LANGDON: What is it?

> (*He goes over.*)

FIRST POLICEMAN: Famous people without their clothes on. Celebrity nudes.

SECOND POLICEMAN: Jesus, look at her.

LANGDON: What d'you mean?

> (*He frowns, not understanding. The* YOUNG POLICEWOMAN, *keeping her distance, looks disapprovingly.*)

SECOND POLICEMAN: Celebrity nudes! Here, look, here's
     Jackie Kennedy . . .
POLICEWOMAN: All women.
FIRST POLICEMAN: Yup.
POLICEWOMAN: No men.
SECOND POLICEMAN: Is that meant to be Britt Ekland?
FIRST POLICEMAN: It's a very bad likeness. I think he must
     have been in the bushes . . .
     (*They laugh. The* POLICEWOMAN *stands alone.*)
POLICEWOMAN: Men would be taking the joke much too far.
     (LANGDON *has picked up a large bunch of flowers, which are
     on the counter. The* POLICEWOMAN *passes on her way out, her
     anger still in her voice.*)
     You don't need to take flowers.
LANGDON: I can't explain. I just thought I would.

50. INT. SCHOOL. DAY
JEAN *moves down the corridor to her classroom. An effort of will to
come in today. She listens to the familiar sounds of the teachers and
children, each in their classes. As she approaches her door,* ROGER
comes out, rather to her surprise. And he is surprised to see her.
ROGER: Oh, Jean . . . I'm sorry. I was settling your class. We
     weren't expecting you.
JEAN: I decided I'd feel better if I came in.
ROGER: I gave them some books and told them to shut up.
JEAN: Good.
     (*He looks at her, not knowing what to say.*)
ROGER: Well . . . you must come round to dinner.
JEAN: Yes, I'd like to.
ROGER: I mean, we must have you back. We don't see enough
     of you.
     (*He looks at her a moment, curiously. Then nods a little and
     backs off down the corridor.*)
     Bye.

51. INT. CLASSROOM. DAY
The class is quiet, all reading, as JEAN *comes in and puts her books
down on the desk. She forestalls all questions by her manner.*

42

JEAN: Right, come on, heads out of books, please everyone.
      That's not how I teach – as you know.
GIRL: Mr Braithwaite said you weren't coming in.
JEAN: Well, then, you have a pleasant surprise. Board, please,
      Marjorie.
GIRL: Please, Miss, I didn't hand in my exercise book.
      (*A* GIRL *gets up to wipe the board.*)
JEAN: Shut up, sit down, open the window.
PUPIL: (*Calling from the back of the class*) You've still got a fag in
      your mouth.
      (JEAN *stops, smiles and takes it out. This little cabaret has put
      everyone at their ease.*)
JEAN: Now. Good. Today we address the question: is
      Shakespeare worth reading although it's only about kings?

52. INT. SCHOOL. DAY
The bell goes. The corridors are thronged with people. JEAN *comes
through the crowd as they go to the playground. Then she turns down a
corridor to where the locker room is. There in a darkened corner* SUZIE
BANNERMAN *is staring into the eyes of a fellow pupil, a* BOY *of 16.
They have been kissing.* JEAN *stops, unseen.* JEAN *looks a moment.
Then the* BOY *moves his hand on to* SUZIE's *skirt between her legs.*
JEAN, *unnoticed, turns to go back the way she came.*

53. EXT. JEAN'S HOUSE. DAY
Sitting outside the house in the sun on the doorstep is a GIRL *of 19,
in duffel coat and jeans. She is reading a paperback.* JEAN *has
returned from school with a lot of exercise books. And is standing
now at the garden gate. The* GIRL *looks up, aware of Jean's gaze.*
KAREN: I'm sorry. I don't mean to surprise you.
JEAN: It's all right.
KAREN: I should have rung.
      (JEAN *can now see her clearly as she has got up. She is pale,
      very slight and unassertive.*)
      I've come from the funeral. I'm a friend of John Morgan's.
      (*There is a silence, as if* JEAN *is bracing herself for the next
      wave of unhappiness. Then she moves towards the house.*)
JEAN: Come in.

54. INT. KITCHEN. DAY

KAREN *is sitting at the kitchen table, she is talking in a rather careless and withdrawn sort of way, without much purpose.* JEAN *is making tea, keeping busy, but attentive to everything* KAREN *says.*

KAREN: I had a kind of inkling he might do something silly. I always thought he was weird.

JEAN: Were you at the same university?

KAREN: He was postgraduate. I'm just first-year.

JEAN: Had you . . .

(JEAN *pauses. We are with her by the cooker.*)

. . . been going out with him?

KAREN: No. I never slept with him. We went to the cinema twice. We'd seen the film about the Indian.

JEAN: *Gandhi?*

KAREN: That's right. Afterwards he couldn't stop talking. He thought this, he thought that. The philosophy of non-violence and so on. And I really didn't think anything. Except obviously the film was very long. In that way we weren't even suited. I think he was trying to impress me.

(JEAN *smiles. She sets out fine china.*)

JEAN: He chose the wrong way.

KAREN: I like people who just are themselves. Not talking rubbish all the time.

(JEAN *looks at her, curious.*)

I know I shouldn't say that about anyone who's dead. But anyone who did what he did to you . . .

JEAN: It certainly upset me.

KAREN: Yes. I can tell.

(*There's a pause.*)

Then he started to pester me. I had to go to his professor to ask him to stop watching me. The worst was in the laundrette.

(JEAN *is watching her, quite still.*)

I think it was me he wanted to do it to. And just by bad luck he did it to you.

(*The two women look at each other, suddenly close in their thoughts. But, as if fearing this closeness,* KAREN *turns away after a moment.* JEAN *has a teapot in her hand.*)

JEAN: Are you going back?

KAREN: When?

JEAN: This evening.

KAREN: Oh, I don't really have any plan. I only came over on an
impulse. Then a policeman at the funeral gave me a lift.

JEAN: Who was that?

KAREN: He was called Langdon. I'd never have thought of it. It
was his idea I should come.

55. INT. SPARE ROOM. DAY

The curtains are drawn in the spare room, which could not be barer.
A bed unmade, no sheets. A simple table at the side. JEAN *is*
standing there as KAREN *comes in. They stand a moment.*

KAREN: Yes, it's nice.

56. INT. JEAN'S HOUSE. DAY

KAREN *has a big plate of sausages and beans and toast in front of*
her. She is shovelling it in happily. JEAN *is sitting opposite,*
watching. Like a mother and child.

57. INT. JEAN'S HOUSE. NIGHT

Later. JEAN *is at the sink washing up.* KAREN *is sitting in an*
armchair at the other side of the room.

JEAN: So how long did you know him?

KAREN: Who?

JEAN: John Morgan.

KAREN: Oh, him. I don't know.

(JEAN *looks across.* KAREN's *mind is elsewhere.*)

Do you have a television?

JEAN: Yes. I have one somewhere. Oh, I keep it under those
books. (*Points to a pile of books and cardboard boxes in the*
corner.) I hardly ever watch it.

KAREN: I watch it most evenings.

JEAN: Even at university? You watch it at university?

KAREN: They have a room you can sit in. (*Leaning over the back*
of the chair) Do you mind if I get it out?

58. INT. JEAN'S HOUSE. NIGHT

KAREN *sits watching a television comedy show. She is perfectly content.*

59. INT. JEAN'S HOUSE. NIGHT

Later. Now only the small light is on beside the armchair where JEAN *sits alone, reading. The door leading upstairs opens and* KAREN *comes out. She is wearing only a vest and pants and her hair is wet from the bath. Silently, she walks right past* JEAN *to the kitchen, collects a pair of nail scissors, and walks back past her.*

KAREN: I've finished in the bathroom. Good night.

(*She goes out.*)

60. INT. LANGDON'S BATHROOM. NIGHT

MIKE LANGDON *stretched out in his bath. He has put the shaving light on, so he is barely lit. On the chair beside him, the black suit is folded with shirt and black tie. We think he is alone. But now a hand trails in the water by his knee. Crouched beside the bath on her knees is a blonde* GIRL *in her mid-twenties, pretty, slightly bland. There is light behind her, so all we have is an impression of blonde hair and warmth. We can tell she's just woken up.*

CHRISSIE: How was the funeral?

LANGDON: Ghastly. I had to go to Derby. And it started to rain. Only his mother left alive. She had no idea why he'd done it.

CHRISSIE: It seems as if neither do you.

(*He smiles, acknowledging this.*)

LANGDON: Have you been riding?

CHRISSIE: Uh-huh. It's why I fell asleep. We broke in a new horse. So I'm saddle-sore.

(*They both smile.*)

LANGDON: The problem is no crime has been committed. Killing yourself is legal. Even in front of somebody else.

CHRISSIE: Yes. Unless she did something to provoke him.

LANGDON: Yes.

(*There's a silence.* CHRISSIE *gets up and goes out of the bathroom, so* LANGDON *has to call out:*)

She'd only known him twenty-four hours.

46

(*No reply.*)

She is – what? – a teacher, a spinster, well loved, obviously good at her job. Lives alone. Loved by her pupils. Did she teach you?

(CHRISSIE *has reappeared with a large white towel which she now holds out.*)

CHRISSIE: No, but I remember her. She was nice.

(LANGDON *does not move.*)

LANGDON: A good woman chosen for some reason as the victim of the ultimate practical joke.

61. INT. JEAN'S HOUSE. NIGHT

Flashback. The beginning of the dinner party. ROGER *and* VERITY *are already seated in armchairs.* MARCIA *leads into the room, her present for* JEAN *under her arm. Then* JEAN *follows, beckoning* MORGAN *into the room.* STANLEY *will be last to arrive.*

VERITY: I don't watch that. I watch that thing on Sundays.

MARCIA: Hello, darling.

VERITY: Roger won't watch it because he says it's full of jokes about Blacks.

ROGER: Marcia. Hello. Stanley.

(ROGER *has stood up to kiss* MARCIA, *and shake hands with* STANLEY. MARCIA *has already ducked down to kiss* VERITY, *who is not to be stopped in her train.* JEAN *has gone straight to her cooking, worried it is overheating, and we are with her now.*)

JEAN: Whoops, I need some more wine.

(*She heads back through the room.* STANLEY *holds out the bottle he has brought.*)

No, red, it's for cooking.

(*She smiles at* MORGAN *as she goes out of the room to the corridor for more. He smiles back, standing alone at the side of the room.*)

ROGER: I didn't say that, it's just that particular *kind* of joke about Blacks . . .

VERITY: I think if they want to be part of things, if they want to be accepted as British, then they have to put up with the fact they will be a butt of people's humour. Just like mothers-in-law.

47

(MORGAN *has gone over to look at Jean's books on the shelves, by himself.* STANLEY *has taken his wine over to the kitchen.*)

STANLEY: (*Muttering,* sotto voce, *to* MARCIA) Do you know who that bloke is?

MARCIA: Stanley, don't be rude. He's a friend of Jean's.

(JEAN *has returned with wine, which she gives to* STANLEY *to open.*)

JEAN: Here you are. Will you open that for me? Roger, do you know John?

ROGER: (*Uncertainly*) Yea . . . gh.

JEAN: This is Verity.

(MORGAN *smiles.*)

VERITY: And if you actually *don't* make jokes about Blacks it's a kind of reverse discrimination. It's a way of saying they don't really belong.

ROGER: No, you have to say . . .

VERITY: I don't *have* to say anything.

(MARCIA *has got a glass of white wine and is now moving to sit down and join in.*)

MARCIA: It's actually Jews who make jokes about Jews. When they do, for some reason, it's called Jewish humour . . .

ROGER: Marcia . . .

MARCIA: . . . but when we do it, it's called anti-Semitism. (*Smiles cheerfully at* MORGAN.) Don't you agree?

(JEAN *looks up from her cooking.* MORGAN *is watching her now from the far side of the room.*)

ROGER: You do realize this is an emotional argument?

VERITY: So?

MARCIA: (*Helping herself to hummus and pitta*) I'll be fined at Weight Watchers!

ROGER: It has no basis in logic at all.

VERITY: Oh, logic.

ROGER: Yes, you know, *logic*, that holds society together. *Logic*, that says people mustn't be allowed to go round killing each other . . .

STANLEY: Quite right.

ROGER: And that also tells you – please, I've started so please let me finish . . .

48

MARCIA: Magnus Magnusson!

ROGER: Logic also tells you that there must be constraints, and that if everyone went round saying what they truly feel, the result would be barbarism. (*Looks round the room. Quietly*) And I prefer civilization. That's all.

(*There is a silence.* ROGER *smiles at* STANLEY *as if to say, 'There we are, that says it all.'* JEAN *is looking across at* MORGAN *who has not lowered his stare throughout this exchange. And now, in the silence,* JEAN *walks to him with a glass of wine.* VERITY *starts again, low, much more bitter.*)

VERITY: Roger dislikes anyone being allowed to express themselves. He sees it as a threat to property values.

ROGER: Darling, I don't think that's quite fair.

(JEAN *is staring at* MORGAN, *astonished by the evenness and boldness of his look.*)

VERITY: He won't allow a firework display on the common for fear a rocket lands on our thatched roof.

ROGER: Darling, now you're raising quite a different point.

VERITY: (*Suddenly shouting at him*) Life is *dangerous*. Don't you realize? And sometimes there's nothing you can do.

(ROGER *is embarrassed. Everyone looks away.*)

ROGER: That's not true. I think you can always limit the danger.

STANLEY: (*Smiling*) What do you say, John Morgan? Speak up. Intercede. It's a marriage. You must adjudicate between warring parties.

(JEAN *looks across to see what* MORGAN *will say. His tone is as level as ever.*)

MORGAN: Well, I can see both sides, I suppose.

62. INT. BEDROOM. NIGHT

The present. LANGDON *is sitting naked on the side of the bed.*
CHRISSIE, *in her dressing gown, is wrapped round his middle, curled up. Only the bathroom light falls across the bed.*

LANGDON: If I said now, 'Go to Derek, divorce him . . .'

CHRISSIE: Oh, Mike . . .

LANGDON: Isn't it logical?

CHRISSIE: Aren't we happy . . .

LANGDON: Of course.

CHRISSIE: . . . as we are?

(*He takes her hand. She smiles.*)

Let's leave it. You spoil things if you push them too hard.

63. INT. BEDROOM. NIGHT

JEAN *lying awake in bed, her eyes wide open. After a silence she gets up and goes to the door, listening, silence.*

64. INT. LANDING. NIGHT

JEAN *stands in her nightdress on the landing. She pushes the door of the spare room open. Inside,* KAREN *is tucked up, fast asleep.* JEAN *looks at her from the door.*

65. INT. JEAN'S ROOM. NIGHT

Flashback, 1953. At exactly the same angle as the previous shot, we see JIM *lying in a bed in the same place as Karen's. His eyes are closed.*

YOUNG JEAN: Jim. Jim, it's hopeless.

> (*We now see she is sitting on the radiator at the other side of the room, her books on the desk in front of her. She wears a dressing gown. She looks very thin and young.*)

JIM: What?

YOUNG JEAN: How can it work any more? Snatching time when my mum's out at cards, knowing we can't get married because of your parents.

JIM: We'll get married.

YOUNG JEAN: Eventually, yes. When you finally get back from Malaya. But it's so long. It makes everything seem pointless. Don't you think we should be sensible?

> (*There's a pause.* JIM *throws back the cover, crosses the room and kneels in front of her. He opens the two sides of her dressing gown, lovingly. She is naked underneath. He looks into her eyes.*)

JIM: No.

66. INT. JEAN'S HOUSE. NIGHT

The present. KAREN *is sitting in the armchair doing nothing. In the front of the frame,* JEAN *is turning on a side lamp. She walks briskly across the room.*

JEAN: What do you think? Would you like to do something? Is there something you'd really like to do? I noticed there's a concert.

KAREN: No.

> (JEAN *has reached the other end of the room and turns.*)

JEAN: Karen, I feel there's a lot you'd like to tell me.

KAREN: Not specially.

JEAN: And sometimes you can't get it out.

> (*There is a silence.* KAREN *says nothing.* JEAN *moves back, speaking very quietly, defeated.*)

Yes. If you like I'll watch television with you.

67. EXT. STREET. NIGHT

Leeds. A darkened street. Rain. A WOMAN *is struggling along the street bent against the rain. It is* JEAN. *In the darkness we can just make out the shape of the buildings – the old high arches and redbrick of the corn exchanges. A single lamp burns in an archway. Then she passes a huge piece of plate glass, with green and red light shining behind it, and steam running down it. The window of a large Chinese restaurant. She walks past, her head down. But then she turns back.*

68. INT. CHINESE RESTAURANT. NIGHT

Inside the restaurant is huge, with very bare tables at great distances. In the corner, some chefs are cooking in an open area with woks. JEAN *is sitting by herself, her face still wet, as if she has just dabbed it dry with a tissue, her wet coat behind her on the chair. At a large circular table some forty feet away from her, in the corner, a Chinese family are eating a cheerful meal. She watches them. They are very animated. She seems thoughtful. Then she looks up and* MIKE LANGDON *has come in with* CHRISSIE.

JEAN: Oh, well, goodness . . .

LANGDON: How are you? This is a coincidence. Do you know Chrissie? Jean Travers.

CHRISSIE: Hello.

    (*She is standing smiling beside him, and now reaches out her hand.* JEAN *smiles.*)

JEAN: (*Lightly*) Hello. Is this coincidence?

LANGDON: Good Lord, yes, I've given up thinking about you.

    (*There is a moment's pause. Then she gestures towards her table.*)

JEAN: Well, do please, yes. Or would I be interrupting?

LANGDON: Not in the slightest.

    (*They sit down at her table.*)

    Chrissie came into Leeds to pick up some gear.

CHRISSIE: I ride horses.

LANGDON: So I said I'd take her in, and we'll go to the cinema.

    (*To the* WAITRESS, *who is handing him a menu*) Yes, thank you.

CHRISSIE: Beer, please.

LANGDON: And me. And what are you doing?

JEAN: Oh, I don't know. (*Smiles at him.*) I've already ordered.

LANGDON: All right.

    (*He nods at the* WAITRESS *who goes. There is a moment.* JEAN *is looking at him as if deciding whether she can trust him. Then she goes ahead.*)

JEAN: I'm afraid I got frightened.

LANGDON: Frightened?

JEAN: Yes.

CHRISSIE: Are you living on your own?

JEAN: No, I'm not, as it happens. A girl came to stay with me . . .

LANGDON: Oh, she stayed.

JEAN: Yes. (*To* CHRISSIE) A friend of John Morgan's. Have you heard about this? So you know who I mean?

(CHRISSIE *nods*.)
Today I just . . . I was going to go home and then somehow I couldn't face it. I just had to get out.

LANGDON: Why does Karen frighten you so much?

(*There's a silence*.)

JEAN: It sounds silly. I just can't get hold of her. She arrived on my doorstep and I thought, oh, she really wants to talk to me. Because she's had a similar experience, I suppose. But it's as if she's missing a faculty. She seems to say something. Then it just slips away. She has no curiosity. (*Shrugs slightly*.) Then also . . . she asked to stay the night. I said, fine. Then next day she didn't leave. Then yesterday she asked if she could stay on.

(LANGDON *is looking straight at her*.)

It's a hard thing to say but I do see how Morgan became obsessed with her.

LANGDON: Did he?

JEAN: Oh, yes. Violently, I think. She's the kind of girl people do become obsessed with.

(*Suddenly* CHRISSIE *gets up*.)

CHRISSIE: Excuse me.

LANGDON: Why don't you just ask her to go?

JEAN: That's what I mean. She makes you feel that would be very rude.

69. INT./EXT. CAR. NIGHT

It is still raining. JEAN *is sitting in the front of Mike Langdon's car. She has wound her window down for fresh air.* CHRISSIE *is sitting at the back. The bleak industrial landscape of Leeds. As they draw up at the lights,* JEAN *turns and looks down the rows of abandoned terraced houses. In the middle of the road children have lit a bonfire, and are playing round it with sticks, and smashing bottles. There is a heavy silence between the three of them.*

70. INT. LANDING. NIGHT

KAREN'*s face asleep in bed. Light falls across her face as* JEAN *and* LANGDON *open the door. They stand together on the landing, looking in.* JEAN *smiles, seeing the funny side of it.*

JEAN: Well, I mean, I can hardly wake her and say, 'This is my
friend the policeman, and he offered to come round and tell
you to leave.'
LANGDON: No.
(*She closes the door and edges past him. They are very close.*)
JEAN: I don't know. Everything gets to seem spooky.
(*She turns. It is dark. At the same moment they are aware that
Morgan was once here, alone with* JEAN. LANGDON'*s eyes go
up to the trap in the ceiling.*)
LANGDON: Is that where the tile was?
JEAN: Yes.
LANGDON: And he fixed it?
JEAN: What?
(*She frowns a moment.*)
LANGDON: How did he fix it? From the inside?
(*She does not answer. She moves past him and goes on down the
stairs.*)

71. INT. KITCHEN. NIGHT
There is no light on in the kitchen, only moonlight, as JEAN *stands
waiting for* LANGDON, *who appears a moment later. They look at
each other across the kitchen.*
JEAN: Chrissie's waiting.
LANGDON: Yes.
(*There is a silence. Neither of them moves.*)
JEAN: Thank you for driving me home.

72. INT./EXT. CAR. NIGHT
The little vanity light is on in the car, so CHRISSIE'*s face is the only
lit object in the night. A curious effect like an illuminated skull. She
sits, waiting. Then the door of the farmhouse opens for* LANGDON *to
come out. She looks across.*

73. INT. LIBRARY. DAY
Flashback. MARCIA *is sitting working at her desk in the British
Library. It is an enormous open area, in which the only books go by
on trolleys. The place is neon-lit and many people are at work
together.* MARCIA *becomes conscious of a man standing opposite her.*

It is MORGAN, *in his anorak.*

MORGAN: I have a list of books I was hoping to borrow.

MARCIA: I'm sorry. You've been misinformed. This isn't a
lending library, you know.

MORGAN: It's the British Library?

MARCIA: Oh, yes. But we don't lend books, or only under very
special circumstances.

MORGAN: I have a letter from my professor.

(MARCIA *smiles, friendly.*)

MARCIA: I'm afraid that isn't going to be nearly special enough.
(*She returns to her work.* MORGAN *stands his ground.*)

MORGAN: Or just to look at the books, not borrow them . . .

MARCIA: Oh, yes, yes, yes, yes. You can *look* – if you are a
registered user. You need authorization from the Librarian.
(*She smiles and returns to work. The encounter has already
passed from her mind.*)

MORGAN: (*Blankly*) Yes, well I'll get that. Then I'll come back.

74. EXT. LIBRARY. DAY

Flashback. MORGAN *stands waiting outside the library. A modern white block, surrounded by barbed wire, in the middle of a field. There is a distorting mirror at the gate in which* MORGAN *watches a small group of* WOMEN *come down the road. He watches them go by.* MARCIA *is among them. He begins to follow.*

75. EXT. MARCIA'S HOUSE. NIGHT

Flashback. The lit windows of the top floor of Marcia's and Stanley's detached, leafy house. STANLEY *is in one room, changing into a pullover and old shirt, while* MARCIA *is moving from one room to the next, chatting all the time, dealing with her children.* MORGAN *stands watching in the bushes outside.*

76. EXT. MARCIA'S HOUSE. DAY

Flashback. Marcia's car is open outside her house. ROGER *is by it. We are watching* MARCIA *put a final cardboard box full of junk into its boot. She closes it and calls in through the front door:*

MARCIA: I'm off now, Stanley. Don't forget to unthaw their lunch.

(*A* CHILD *appears very briefly, whom* MARCIA *stoops down to kiss. A dog runs out.*)

77. INT. CAR. DAY

Flashback. The car now loaded. MARCIA *and* ROGER *side by side.*

MARCIA: It was funny. Clearing out all my stuff began to upset me.

ROGER: Really?

MARCIA: Don't you feel that?

ROGER: The past, you mean? (*Takes a shrewd look at her.*) That isn't like you.

(*There is a silence between them.*)

MARCIA: Second-hand clothes . . .

(ROGER *turns back.*)

ROGER: They say that murderers are drawn to the second-hand.

MARCIA: I hadn't heard that.

ROGER: Yes, there's a book . . .

MARCIA: You like murder, Roger.

ROGER: Yes, oh God, yes, I'm addicted. Yes, there's a theory
that murder is characteristically committed by people who
handle other people's things. In second-hand clothes shops,
junk shops, markets.
(*He takes a quick look at her, but she is not reacting.*)
Self-improvement, that's another hallmark. People who
teach themselves things, at home, at night, theories they
only half understand. Informal education. A fantasy life of
singular intensity.

MARCIA: Didn't you go to Switzerland last year?

ROGER: Oh, yes . . . I . . . yes, a package tour. To the
Reichenbach Falls. There were forty of us from all over
England. To see where Moriarty pushed Sherlock Holmes
over. Wonderful countryside.

MARCIA: What did Verity think?

ROGER: Ah. She didn't come with me. No.
(*There's a pause.*)
A colleague from Home Economics came along.
(*There is a notable grimmer air to* MARCIA *as she swings the car
round towards the church hall.* ROGER *tries to break the mood.*)
Do you like murder?

MARCIA: Not much. But I prefer it to romance.

78. INT. JUMBLE SALE. DAY

Flashback. MARCIA *is working at a stall in a busy jumble sale
taking place in a church hall. Stalls with jams and cakes and toys.*
MARCIA *working at the second-hand clothes stall. The other helpers
are laughing with her at some clothes too bad even for the sale.*
MORGAN *in his anorak is at the other end of the room, pretending to
examine some toys, but sneaking looks at* MARCIA. MARCIA *is seen
from* MORGAN'*s point of view to be nodding vigorously, in
agreement with a customer. Then she takes a pound note which she
needs to get changed and crosses the room to the other side with it.
The camera follows from* MORGAN'*s point of view.*

There, at the other side, JEAN *is supervising a model desert into
which you have to stick a pin to guess where the buried treasure is.*
MORGAN *watches as* MARCIA *gets change from* JEAN, *but as*
MARCIA *goes back to her stall,* MORGAN'*s stare stays on* JEAN, *who*

is now smiling and handing a pin to a little boy. She is quite oblivious of MORGAN *at the other end. He looks content. He has found what he is looking for.*

79. INT. SCHOOL HALL. NIGHT
The present. JEAN *up a ladder adjusting a light for a small stage, which is at one end of the school hall. Four hundred seats have been set out, empty.* JEAN *has a cigarette in her mouth and her jeans on. She looks entirely in her element. She loves this work. The stage lights point at a medieval set. The light is hot, so she burns her hand, but she's used to it. In the back row,* KAREN *sits alone, four hundred empty seats in front of her.*

80. INT. SCHOOL. NIGHT
The school play. The hall now packed for the performance. The set on stage is black curtains with turrets and a landing place. Two boys

in Renaissance costume – one with black headgear and statesman's robes, the other in the plain brown smock of a boatman. The lighting is full of colour – deep yellows and reds. The thickness and warmth of the atmosphere in the hall, plus the thickness of their make-up, gives the colours a lovely density.

'BOATMAN': The river flows dark tonight, Sir Thomas. Will you get on my boat?

'SIR THOMAS': Boatman, although I do not mean to deny you your livelihood I cannot take your boat. If I travel tonight, I will travel to the tower.

'BOATMAN': They say that is a place from which no man escapes.

'SIR THOMAS': Nay, not alive. But, boatman, we are set here on earth to do God's will, and if I do it tonight and in the fullness of my heart, he shall protect me, and lead me to a better place than any that we have known in this world.

'BOATMAN': Well, I wish you good fortune, sire.

'SIR THOMAS': I thank you. You are lucky to know no kings. (*Takes out a gold sovereign.*) Here, take gold. (*Hands it over.*)

Remember me in your prayers.
(*We go high above the hall as the curtains close and there is solid, warm and heartfelt applause.*)

81. INT. SCHOOL HALL. NIGHT
The chairs are all higgledy-piggledy, because PARENTS *and* TEACHERS *are having a reception in the body of the hall.* PARENTS *and* TEACHERS *stand in knots drinking wine or Coca-cola. Trays of food from the cookery classes go round. Right by the stage* KAREN *is being quizzed by a parent,* MR VARLEY, *who has gone up to her, seeing her standing alone.*

MR VARLEY: So who are you, my dear?

KAREN: Oh, I'm a friend of Miss Travers.

MR VARLEY: We all love Jean Travers. She's a wonderful character.

KAREN: Yes.
(*She smiles nervously and tries to look away.*)

MR VARLEY: So what do you do?

KAREN: Oh . . .
(*She shrugs and blushes.*)

MR VARLEY: What? Come on, answer. What's this? Too proud to talk to me?
(*She looks desperately across to where* JEAN *is seen to be in conversation with a couple of* PARENTS. *Their* DAUGHTER *is in Renaissance costume beside them.*)
Who are you? What do you do?
(*She moves away, but as she does, he reaches out and grabs her lightly by the arm.*)
Now look . . .
(*At the other side of the hall.* JEAN *in conversation with the* PARENTS.)

PARENTS: (*Alternately*) I won't want Janice to do A level English. Physics, that's the thing. We want her to get on. We bought her a home computer. We don't let her buy games. No *Star Wars*, nothing like that. ICI needs physicists, doesn't it?
(JEAN'*s attention has gone to where* KAREN *has now dropped her drink on the floor, her face red.* MR VARLEY *is now trying*)

to put a hand on her in a gesture of reassurance, but she is recoiling.)

JEAN: Excuse me.

(*JEAN joins another* TEACHER *on her way to the incident. Another* PARENT *has joined in, trying physically to restrain* MR VARLEY.)

What on earth's going on?

TEACHER: It's one of the parents.

JEAN: How is it possible?

(*Now there are raised voices.* KAREN *is about to cry. The* HELPFUL PARENT's *voice carries over the party.*)

HELPFUL PARENT: Leave her! Leave her alone!

KAREN: (*Shouts:*) I wasn't saying anything. I didn't do anything!

(MR VARLEY *blunders away through the party, bumping into people in a blind hurry to get out. The* TEACHER *shouts at his departing back:*)

TEACHER: Come back, Mr Varley – please.

(JEAN *looks across at* KAREN.)

JEAN: Come on.

82. INT. SCHOOL CORRIDOR. NIGHT

JEAN *and* KAREN *come quickly down the corridor, which is not lit, towards Jean's classroom.* KAREN *has cut her hand on the glass.*

JEAN: What did he say?

KAREN: I don't know. What difference does it make? Why can't people leave me *alone*?

83. EXT. TOWER BLOCK. NIGHT

Flashback. The tower block at the University of Essex stands gaunt against the sky. More like a housing estate than a university. From one uncurtained window a light shines out. MORGAN *sitting at his desk, twelve floors up in the air.*

84. EXT. UNIVERSITY. NIGHT

Flashback. A gulch of tower blocks. They stand, lined up, sinister, desolated. Scraps of paper blow down between them. A scene more like urban desolation than a university. Concrete stanchions, deserted. A roadsign-like tin plate saying 'Keynes 2. Nightline' with an arrow.

85. EXT./INT. STUDENT CANTEEN. NIGHT

*Flashback. Glass on both sides, so we can see right through –
A few lonely* STUDENTS *at the plastic tables.*

86. INT. TOWER BLOCK. NIGHT

*Flashback. An empty lift automatically opens its doors. Inside it is
painted blue. Someone has scrawled, 'Fuck you All'.*

87. INT. KAREN'S ROOM. NIGHT

*Flashback. Karen's university room is very plainly furnished. A
single light is on on the desk. There is a bed and a couple of posters,
some books on the desk. We are behind* KAREN *as she moves towards
bed, taking off her top. She gets into bed in pants and vest. She turns
her light off.*

88. INT. CLASSROOM. NIGHT

The present. JEAN *has not put the light on, so only the street light
falls into the room, where* JEAN *is dabbing Dettol on to* KAREN*'s
hand with some cotton wool she has got from the classroom medicine
cupboard. When she speaks, it is very quietly.*

JEAN: What did he want?

KAREN: Who?

JEAN: That parent.

KAREN: Nothing. He just asked questions.

JEAN: What kind?

> (KAREN *is sulking, only just audible.*)

KAREN: Oh, you know, who was I? What was I doing here?

> (JEAN *looks at her, as if at last beginning to understand her.*)

JEAN: It sounds quite innocent.

KAREN: It's just that I hate it. All this asking that goes on.
People digging about. The way people have to dig in each
other. It's horrible.

> (JEAN *nods. She puts the kidney bowl aside. It is a little red
> from* KAREN*'s blood.*)

JEAN: Did you say that to Morgan?

KAREN: Yes, well, I did.

JEAN: No wonder. I think you drove Morgan crazy.

> (KAREN *looks at her mistrustfully.*)

KAREN: I don't know what you mean.

JEAN: No, well, exactly. That's why.

> (KAREN *looks away.*)
>
> Goodness, I'm not saying *deliberately*, I don't mean you meant to . . .

KAREN: I don't do anything! I don't say anything!

> (KAREN *looks for a moment fiercely at* JEAN.)

89. INT. CORRIDOR. NIGHT

Flashback. A screwdriver working at a lock. MORGAN *is on his knees in the corridor outside Karen's room, unscrewing the entire lock. The wood squeals slightly under the pressure. Then lock, handle, plate, all come away in his hand. He looks a moment through the hole in the door that is left. Then he pushes the door open.*

90. INT. KAREN'S ROOM. NIGHT

Flashback. We approach the bed. MORGAN *steps in front of us and kneels down beside it.*

MORGAN: Karen. Karen. It's me.

> (*An eye opens. Then, in panic, she wakes.*)
>
> Karen, listen to me, please.

KAREN: Get out of here!

MORGAN: I only want to talk to you.

> (*She gets up and runs along the bed. From the desk at the end she starts picking up books and throwing them at him.*)

KAREN: Fuck you! Get out!

MORGAN: No, look, please, you must listen to me . . .

> (*He grabs at her. They struggle and fall to the floor, her head cracking as she goes down. Instinctively he lets go and she scrambles out from under him, like an animal in panic. She starts shouting.*)
>
> I want some feeling! I want some contact! I want you fucking near me!
>
> (*She picks up the typewriter from the desk and throws it at him. It slams into his chest with a terrible thud.*)

KAREN: Get out of here.

91. INT. CLASSROOM. NIGHT

The present. KAREN *passes* JEAN *on her way out of the classroom.*
JEAN *grabs at her wrist as she goes by.*

JEAN: Please don't go.

KAREN: You make an effort, you try to be nice, try to do
anything . . . you just get your head chopped off. Why *try*?
(*Looks angrily at* JEAN, *like a little girl*.) Anyway, tell me, go
on, tell me, since you're so clever, what did *you* do?

JEAN: Karen . . .
KAREN: If it wasn't an accident, I'd love to know what *you* did.
    (*She turns and runs out of the room.*)
JEAN: Karen. Karen. Come back!

92. INT. CORRIDOR. NIGHT
The corridor deserted. KAREN *has run away and into the night.*
Another corridor, also deserted. A third.

93. INT. HALL. NIGHT
The school hall, now empty and darkened. The chairs all over the
place. JEAN *comes in, stands a moment. But there is no one there.*

94. INT. MARCIA'S ROOM. NIGHT
Flashback, 1953. YOUNG MARCIA *is sitting on the bed in her*

dressing gown in a room much more feminine in its decoration than Young Jean's. Very fifties. The effect is made odd by the bottles of light ale they are both holding. YOUNG JEAN *is on the other side of the room in her coat.*

YOUNG JEAN: (*Quietly*) If I had the guts I'd just say to him, 'Look, I don't want you to go, I need you.'

YOUNG MARCIA: Why don't you say that?

YOUNG JEAN: Because to him, it's everything. Being an airman is everything. Until he gets to Malaya he isn't going to feel being an airman is real.

YOUNG MARCIA: And what do you feel?

YOUNG JEAN: I don't know. Of course, I don't like it . . .

YOUNG MARCIA: Are you frightened he's going to get killed?

(JEAN *looks at her in astonishment.*)

YOUNG JEAN: No. No, of course not. I hadn't even thought of it. Why do you say that?

68

YOUNG MARCIA: I'm sorry. I didn't think.
  (*There's a pause.*)
YOUNG JEAN: If you want the truth it's this: with him I can't
    talk. With him I can't say anything I feel. Because . . .
    because I read books I feel for some reason I'm not allowed
    to talk. For that reason, there is always a gulf. (*Crosses the
    room and puts her empty bottle down.*) It doesn't seem a very
    good basis for marriage.
YOUNG MARCIA: No. I suppose.
  (JEAN *goes and embraces* MARCIA, *in fondness.* MARCIA
  smiles too.)
  (*Tentatively*) Perhaps . . . perhaps sex isn't everything.
YOUNG JEAN: No.
  (JEAN *grins widely. They both burst out laughing at the
  unlikeliness of this statement.*)
YOUNG MARCIA: It's time that you talked to him.
YOUNG JEAN: Soon he'll be gone.

95. INT. LANGDON'S HOUSE. DAY

CHRISSIE *is standing in the bathroom, looking in the mirror. She
stands a moment, then smiles, as if in affection for everything around
her. Then she turns and goes into the bedroom. A suitcase, already
nearly full, is open on the bed. She looks at it a moment. The phone
beside the bed begins to ring. She pauses a moment, then goes to the
chest of drawers to get more stuff to put in the suitcase.*

96. EXT. LANGDON'S HOUSE. DAY

Outside a MAN *is waiting in a Land-Rover. As he watches her close
the door, he gets out of the car. He is about 50, bald, countrified, in
green Huskie jacket and wellingtons.* CHRISSIE *comes down the
path.*

97. INT. LANGDON'S OFFICE. DAY

LANGDON *is sitting in his office at the police station. He has the
phone to his ear. It is ringing out. He looks up and the*
POLICEWOMAN *who was at the house on the day of the suicide is
standing there.*
POLICEWOMAN: There's a man out here to see you.

(LANGDON *nods and puts down the phone. He goes out into the main office and goes to the desk. On the other side, a man is sitting, his coat wrapped over his knee. It is* ROGER BRAITHWAITE. *He looks up.*)

98. INT. JEAN'S HOUSE. NIGHT
JEAN *sitting by herself in the dark watching television. It is a discussion programme.*
CHAIRMAN: (*On the screen*) And so what would you say we mean by lying?
BEARDED MAN: (*On the screen*) Well, it's not telling the truth. At its most basic. Or at least not telling what we believe to be the truth. That's lying. But there's also a kind of lying by omission, failing to say something which is clear to us, leaving something unsaid, which we know we ought to say.

Which is in a way morally an equal crime.
(*There is a knock at the door.* JEAN *turns, slightly dazed. She touches the switch of her remote-control unit.*)

CHAIRMAN: (*On the screen*) But do you think . . .
(*He goes to silence.* JEAN *turns on a lamp. She opens the door,* LANGDON *is standing there.*)

LANGDON: Hello. How are you?
(*She looks at him a moment.*)

JEAN: You look pretty shattered.

LANGDON: Yes.
(*She lets him in, then goes to the television to turn it off. Pictures of Nixon at his most triumphant, arms above head, briefly seen before she kills it.*)
I'm afraid I've had trouble at home. Chrissie went back to her husband.

JEAN: She had one already?

LANGDON: Oh, yes. Who she told me she never saw any more. But all the time – I don't know – it turns out I was a sub-plot. The real story was happening elsewhere.

JEAN: That's a terrible feeling.

LANGDON: The worst.

(*There's a slight pause.*)

It's shaken my whole idea of myself. What I'm doing as a policeman. If the day was no good, if it was awful or silly, I could always go back to Chrissie and laugh. But now it turns out, she wasn't really with me. She laughed. But she was elsewhere.

JEAN: What's he like?

LANGDON: Awful. He's the sort of man who keeps sheep. I mean, for God's sake, if you want wool, go and buy it in a shop.

(JEAN *stands a moment, not knowing what to say.*)

Listen . . . I'll tell you why I'm here. I was piecing together the evening . . .

JEAN: Oh God, can't you leave it?

(LANGDON *is surprised by her sudden rudeness.*)

LANGDON: Well, yes. This is just an amateur's interest.

JEAN: All right.

(*She nods, allowing him to go on.*)

LANGDON: It's just . . . there was food and then there was talking. Then you went upstairs. Didn't you have a few moments alone with him? You were together. What did you talk about?

JEAN: Fixing the roof.

(*There is a pause.*)

LANGDON: It's just Roger . . . your colleague . . . Roger says when you came back he remembers you'd changed.

JEAN: Changed?

LANGDON: Not, I don't mean, I'm not saying as a person. Your clothes.

JEAN: I put on trousers. I'd snagged my stocking. (*Moves away. Cheerfully*) Would you like some tea? Gosh, poor you, so how are you managing alone?

(*But his gaze is steady.*)

LANGDON: Don't you think you should tell me?

JEAN: What?

LANGDON: What happened? Was it your fault?

(*She looks at him nervously, trapped at last. Then she goes and sits on the sofa. Her shoulders sag, as if the whole effort of the last weeks were over.*)

JEAN: I think, in a way, it's because he was a stranger. I'm not sure I can explain. Because I didn't know him, now I feel him dragging me down. I thought I could get over it. But everywhere now . . . the darkness beckons. (*Looks across at him.*) These things become real. He wants me down there.

LANGDON: Well, you have to fight.

JEAN: I've fought. How dare you? (*Suddenly becomes angry,*

beginning to shake) I've fought for three weeks. And you
didn't help. Sending me that miserable little girl. What
gives you that right? To meddle?
(*He doesn't answer.*)
The police who always bring sadness.
(LANGDON's *gaze does not falter.*)
LANGDON: I'm going to sit here. I won't go away.

99. INT. STORE. DAY
Flashback. At once the bell of the shop ringing as JEAN *comes into
the small grocery store.* MR KARANJ *stands behind the delicatessen
counter.* JEAN *goes round, tumbling things into a wire basket.*
MR KARANJ: Ah, you are holding a dinner, Miss Travers.
JEAN: Who told you?
MR KARANJ: The whole town has heard.
  (MR KARANJ *smiles.*)
JEAN: No, just some friends round to supper.
MR KARANJ: Yes. Mrs Pilborough was in.
  (JEAN *passes a man whose face we do not see. He is wearing an
  anorak.*)
  She is taking wine to your dinner. A bottle of Muscadet.
  She asked if I knew what you were cooking.
JEAN: Chicken.
MR KARANJ: Perfect. I felt she was safe.
  (MR KARANJ's *daughter,* SHARMI, *has appeared at the bottom
  of the stairs which lead to their flat above the shop. She stands,
  framed in the doorway, as* JEAN *dumps her goods on the
  counter.*)
JEAN: If I remember anything else, will you send Sharmi round?
MR KARANJ: She cannot leave the shop after dark. She has
  never been out in the evening. Have you, Sharmi?
  (SHARMI *smiles ambiguously.*)
  It is a matter of pride to me. She has never once left her
  home in the dark. (*Turns and addresses her sharply.*) Khari
  kyoa ho. Jao oopar jao.
SHARMI: Jati hoon papaji. Aap ki chai tayar hai. Aap jalli peelo.
  (*She turns and looks at* JEAN, *smiling a second, then she*

74

disappears into the dark upstairs. We travel sideways and see the man whose face we missed. It is MORGAN. *He is watching.*)

JEAN: (*Out of vision*) Thank you. That's all.

100. INT. JEAN'S HOUSE. DAY

Flashback. JEAN *puts her shopping down on the work surface, then turns to the cookbook. It is propped up already. She flips it open. It says 'Coq au vin'.*

101. EXT. JEAN'S HOUSE. EVENING

Flashback. MARCIA *coming up the path to the house with* STANLEY *following. It is evening and the lights are on in the house.* MARCIA *talking as she comes.*

MARCIA: Now, Stanley, don't drink too much, please. Last night you were stupid with gin.

STANLEY: I like gin.

(*As if from the bushes, unremarked,* MORGAN *steps into frame, suddenly beside them, already waiting.*)

MARCIA: Ah.

MORGAN: I rang the bell.

MARCIA: There's no need. She can see us anyway.

(MARCIA, *puzzled for only a second, now taps on the window, and waves vigorously.* JEAN, *her back turned to her cooking, now looks to the window.*)

Hello Jean!

(MORGAN *is smiling at* STANLEY.)

MORGAN: I'm John Morgan.

(JEAN *opens the door welcomingly.*)

JEAN: Ah, hello, hello, you brought an extra.

STANLEY: (*Frowns.*) No.

JEAN: Come in, come in, come on, the more the merrier.

(MORGAN *holds out his hand to* JEAN, *as* MARCIA *sweeps on into the house.* STANLEY *is left with the bottle of wine he has brought.*)

MORGAN: John Morgan.

MARCIA: I've already told Stanley he's not to get drunk.

(*Everyone has moved on into the house, except* STANLEY, *who alone has noticed something odd.*)

STANLEY: What?

102. EXT. AIRFIELD. NIGHT

Flashback, 1953. By one of the dormitory sheds YOUNG JEAN *stands alone. Suddenly a shaft of light falls on the wet pathway and* JIM *steps out, fully dressed in his RAF uniform, carrying his rolled-up luggage, his buckles gleaming, the perfect figure of the airman.*

JIM: Well, what d'you think?

YOUNG JEAN: Well, of course, you look wonderful.

(*There is a moment's pause. They are some way apart.*)

JIM: You don't like me going.

YOUNG JEAN: What makes you say that? I've never said that. I've encouraged you. I can see it's your happiness. You've never been happier than today. I've always told you, you must do what you want.

JIM: Yes. You've supported me. And I've been grateful. I'll come back. We'll have a house.

(*There is a pause.*)

If you want to stop me, you can.

(*She shakes her head.*)

YOUNG JEAN: No, I'll study. I've lots to do.

JIM: Are you being true with me?

YOUNG JEAN: True? What does it mean?

(JIM *waits, serious.*)

JIM: If you've anything to say, speak it now.

(*There are tears in her eyes. She shakes her head.*)

YOUNG JEAN: Nothing.

(*He moves towards her and kisses her.*)

JIM: Goodbye.

(*They begin to walk. We are above them. It is apparently deserted till we turn the corner. All over the rest of the airfield,* AIRMEN *are making their way with bags over their shoulders. Four great planes are waiting.* COMMANDING OFFICERS *with lists of where they're to go.* WIVES *standing waving at the side of the field. The* MEN *thicken into a crowd, going in one direction, till* JEAN *is the only woman among them.* JIM *turns,*

and goes, joining the flow. JEAN *stands alone as the other* MEN *sweep past her. One of the great planes shudders into life, with a roar.* JIM *turns at the steps, and mouths the word 'Adios'. He goes in.* JEAN *stands alone on the pathway, her dress blowing from the propellers. The plane moves towards us.*)

103. INT. JEAN'S HOUSE. NIGHT
Flashback. The dinner party at its most raucous and warmest. A pitch of happy declamation. STANLEY *is suddenly the most vociferous of all.*

STANLEY: Revenge! That's what it is. Revenge! That's what she's doing.

VERITY: Who?

STANLEY: The Prime Minister. Taking some terrible revenge. For something. Some deep damage. Something inside. God

78

knows what. For crimes behind the privet hedge. And now the whole country is suffering. And yet we've done nothing to her.

ROGER: Do you think that?

JEAN: (*Setting the dish down*) Coq au vin.

(*She takes the lid off. It looks fantastic.*)

ROGER: Ah, marvellous.

MARCIA: Stanley, you're drunk.

(JEAN *dishes it out with green salad and French bread.*)

STANLEY: Drunk? Yes. Drunk and disorderly. Where once I was orderly. My thoughts were once in neat rows. Like vegetables. Pegged out, under cloches. I kept my thoughts under cloches. But now they grow wild. (*Turns to* MORGAN.) You wouldn't know, I'm the local solicitor, the town's official sanctifier of greed. Those little unseemly transactions. I see people as they truly are.

MARCIA: Nonsense.

STANLEY: I remember once my father, also a solicitor, said to me, 'I have learnt never to judge any man by his behaviour with money or the opposite sex.' Yet it is my own saddened experience, that those are the *only* ways to judge them.

VERITY: Salad?

STANLEY: Thanks.

(*The hot chicken is variously admired.*)

MARCIA: Stanley thinks good of nobody . . .

STANLEY: Not true. I *expect* good of nobody. And am sometimes pleasantly surprised. And when I find good . . . my first feeling is one of nostalgia. For something we've lost. Ask John Morgan.

(*He turns to* MORGAN. *There's a pause.*)

MORGAN: Well, I don't know. I only know goodness and anger and revenge and evil and desire . . . these seem to me far better words than neurosis and psychology and paranoia. These old words . . . these good old words have a sort of conviction which all this modern apparatus of language now lacks.

(*People have stopped eating and are looking at him. There is a silence.*)

79

MARCIA: Ah, well, yes . . .
MORGAN: We bury these words, these simple feelings, we bury
    them deep. And all the building over that constitutes this
    century will not wish these feelings away.
    (*There is a pause.* JEAN *looks at him. He looks steadily back.*)
ROGER: Well, I mean, you'd have to say what you really mean
    by that.
MORGAN: Would I?
ROGER: Define your terms.
    (MORGAN *looks at him.*)
MORGAN: They don't need defining. If you can't feel them you
    might as well be dead.

104. EXT. CLOUDS. NIGHT
*Flashback, 1953. Totally silent. Model shot. Jim's big troopcarrier
flies through the night. No noise. The dark shape moving through the
clouds.*

105. EXT. AIRFIELD. NIGHT
*Flashback, 1953. Silent also. We crane down from way above the
field as* YOUNG JEAN *walks back, alone. The field now deserted.*

106. INT. JEAN'S HOUSE. NIGHT
Flashback. The dinner party. MORGAN *looks up to the ceiling.*
MORGAN: It looks as if your roof is in trouble. I'm very
    practical.
    (JEAN *looks a moment round the company.*)
JEAN: Right.

107. EXT. STREET. NIGHT
Flashback, 1953. JIM *in a street in Singapore, which is the poor
area, just huts and squatters and roadside lights. He is being as
patient as he can with the attentions of his cockney friend,* ARTHUR,
who pursues him.
JIM: No, get away, I don't want to.
ARTHUR: Is it your girl? Is that what it is?
    (ARTHUR *takes* JIM *by the arm and stops him walking on.*)
    Jim, you're a crazy man. You've got to go to the brothel.

81

You're here for six months, you can't just give up.

JIM: Well, that's what I'll do.

(*He tries to move off, but* ARTHUR *takes his arm again.*)

ARTHUR: There's a good place – listen – off limits. Not a brothel.

JIM: I don't want to go.

ARTHUR: Please, it's . . . it'll be like the local. Only better.

(*He has taken him by the shoulder and now looks him in the eye.*)

Jim. Jim, take me seriously. I can give you a very good time.

(JIM *smiles.* ARTHUR's *humour has won him.*)

JIM: All right. But no fucking.

ARTHUR: I can give you a no fucking good time.

108. EXT. SHACK. NIGHT

Flashback, 1953. A piece of wasteground. On it a single shack, a simple wooden building, with light shaded at its windows. JIM *and* ARTHUR *appear in the foreground.*

ARTHUR: Show me your money.

(JIM *has a roll of notes which he takes from his pocket.* ARTHUR *peels half off and hands it back to him.*)

Put that in your shoe.

(*They both stoop down. They put notes in their shoes. Then stand.*)

Let's go in.

109. INT. JEAN'S HOUSE. NIGHT

Flashback. JEAN *goes up the stairs, leading. It is very dark.* MORGAN *is following behind.* JEAN *stops dead, without looking round.*

JEAN: What you said . . . what you said about those feelings. It did make such sense.

MORGAN: Yes, I thought you'd understand me.

(*He waits a moment. She points to the ladder and trap that lead to the roof.*)

JEAN: It's here.

(MORGAN *moves past her, very close indeed. He goes up the ladder and lifts the trap.* JEAN's *point of view of him from below.*)

110. INT. SHACK. NIGHT

Flashback, 1953. A group of MALAYS *are sitting in a circle, on boxes, in a plain wooden room as* ARTHUR *and* JIM *push open the wooden door. There is no sign of the room having any function but the game. It stops. A* YOUNG MALAY *who is lounging against the wall moves towards them.* ARTHUR *speaks, exaggeratedly, English to the foreigner.*

ARTHUR: Take part in your game. We would like to. We have heard. The best game of poker in Malaya.

(*The* YOUNG MALAY *looks to the group. A* FATTER, OLDER MALAY *nods.*)

YOUNG MALAY: OK.

(*There is silence as* ARTHUR *and* JIM *sit on boxes to join the game. The cards are dealt. Then an opium pipe is passed to* ARTHUR. JIM *tries to warn him, but* ARTHUR *cuts him off.* ARTHUR *accepts unhesitatingly. He begins to smoke. A gesture of brio.*)

ARTHUR: Thanks very much.

111. INT. LANDING. NIGHT

Flashback. MORGAN *comes down the ladder with the torch.* JEAN *waits on the landing. The scene exactly as we saw it earlier.*

JEAN: A slate fell in the night. I was frightened to go up there.

MORGAN: It's all right.

(*He is quite still on the ladder.*)

Shall we go down?

(*He begins to move.*)

112. INT. SHACK. NIGHT

Flashback, 1953. At once ARTHUR *slumps to the floor, passing out from the opium.* JIM *gets up in panic, his crate falling behind him. The* YOUNG MALAY *intercedes.*

YOUNG MALAY: It's OK. It's OK.

JIM: What have you given him?

(*The two* MEN *on either side of* ARTHUR *take hold of his body and start to drag it across the room.*)

YOUNG MALAY: I have something . . . Hold him!

JIM: *DON'T DRAG HIM!*

(*At once* JIM *is restrained as he tries to move across. The* FAT
MALAY *nods at the other* MEN. ARTHUR *is deathly white.*)
Who runs this game? I thought you were the boss.
(*He looks at the* FAT MALAY, *who turns away.*)
YOUNG MALAY: No fighting, please!
(ARTHUR'S *body is pulled at alarming speed behind bead
curtains. The* YOUNG MALAY *is now opposite* JIM.)
I have something. Step in here. I will give you some
medicine for him.
(*He gestures to the bead curtains.* ARTHUR *has vanished behind
them.* JIM'S *face.*)

113. INT. LANDING. NIGHT
Flashback. MORGAN *has reached the bottom of the ladder.* JEAN,
*standing still, suddenly and impetuously grabs at him with her hand
as he is about to move by. It is as if the gesture is suddenly
irresistible, and he turns and embraces her in return. They begin*

frantically clutching at each other's clothes. The feeling is violent,
hysterical. He pulls her down towards the floor.

114. INT. SHACK. NIGHT
Flashback, 1953. JIM, *sweating, looks to the room and begins very*
slowly to walk towards it.

115. INT. LANDING. NIGHT
Flashback. As JEAN *and* MORGAN *go down on the floor, her legs*
slip along the board, catching a nail in the skirting board. Her
stocking rips. At once a thin line of blood.

116. INT. SHACK. NIGHT
Flashback, 1953. JIM *parts the bead curtain. The* YOUNG MALAY
stands opposite him and smiles.
YOUNG MALAY: English airman.
    (*Subliminally, for a moment,* JIM *turns to see* ARTHUR's *body*
    lying on the ground, before he is taken from behind by the
    YOUNG MALAY *who wraps his arm round his throat.*)

117. INT. JEAN'S HOUSE. DAY
Flashback. JEAN *at the sink. We have* MORGAN's *point of view.*
We do not see him. Instead we travel slowly towards JEAN *in a*
movement that approaches her back.
JEAN: I love the slow evenings once the summer begins to come.
    It doesn't get dark until eight.
    (*We move right in on her.*)

118. INT. SHACK. NIGHT
Flashback, 1953. The YOUNG MALAY *passes a knife across* JIM's
throat. Blood pours from the wound.

119. INT. JEAN'S HOUSE. DAY
Flashback. JEAN *looking in amazement at* MORGAN *who is now*
sitting at the table.
JEAN: Absurd! It's impossible!
MORGAN: No.
    (MORGAN *lifts the revolver and blows his brain out.*)

120. INT. SHACK. NIGHT

Flashback, 1953. Repeated action, shown three times: the knife goes back to the beginning of the action each time across JIM'*s throat. Each time blood spurts in a red line across his neck.*

121. DREAM

Process shot: the YOUNG JEAN, *naked, runs down a corridor at full pelt. The walls are on either side of her but as she runs they recede. Her figure stays the same size in proportion to the walls, which go endlessly by. She strains, to no effect.*

122. INT. JEAN'S HOUSE. DAY

Flashback. JEAN *standing at the sink.* MORGAN *sitting at the kitchen table, slumped across, his head blown off.*

123. INT. LANDING. NIGHT

Flashback. MORGAN *is on top of* JEAN, *as if about to make love to*

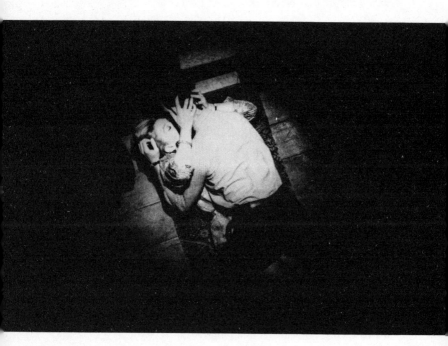

(The GIRL *giggles. Another* GIRL *thinks this the most hilarious thing.)*

JEAN: Has she been in touch with her parents?

GIRL: Oh yes, Miss.

JEAN: Good.

BOY: *(From the back of the class)* She said she couldn't see the point of school.

JEAN: *(Serious, quiet)* No, well, sometimes I have that problem. *(Looks round the class.)* Anyone else? Anyone else want to go?

(There is a silence, profound, as if recognizing her seriousness.) You are free. You are free to go if you wish.

(The whole class seen in wide shot, quite still. Then JEAN *speaks very quietly.)*

Right then, for those of us still remaining—us maniacs,

90

her. *It is very quiet suddenly. Their faces are very close together. We are way above them, and as they speak, we come closer slowly, creeping in. We can only just hear.*

MORGAN: Listen, I know you're in trouble.

JEAN: What?

MORGAN: You're in trouble. Like me.

JEAN: I don't know what you mean.

MORGAN: Come on.

JEAN: No.

MORGAN: You're lonely.

JEAN: Yes, well, I'm lonely, I'm not in trouble.

MORGAN: Please don't argue with me. All that hope coming out of you. All that cheerful resolution. All that wonderful enlightenment. For what? For nothing. You know it's for nothing. Don't tell me that cheerfulness is real.

JEAN: Yes, of course.

MORGAN: You and I—we understand each other.

JEAN: What? No . . . what?

MORGAN: You fake. You fake all that cheerfulness.

JEAN: No, please. It's who I am.

MORGAN: Then why did you lead me up here?

JEAN: I didn't.

MORGAN: Liar! *(He twists her head and speaks into her ear.)* You know. You know where you're looking.

JEAN: I don't.

MORGAN: You've been here. Where I am.

(She begins to struggle free of him, panicking, realizing the extent of his madness. At once he grabs at her sweater, but she wrenches herself free.)

JEAN: I haven't. I'm sorry. I haven't been where you are. I have to change.

(She has struggled up. There is blood running down her stocking.)

MORGAN: No.

JEAN: Yes. *Please.*

(She is about to move towards her room, when he grabs her arm. He looks at her with a sudden, terrifying ferocity.)

MORGAN: *You will.*

87

124. EXT. JEAN'S HOUSE. NIGHT

Flashback. The house seen from a great distance. Lit windows in the night. The front door opens. The end of a dinner party. The sound of STANLEY, *very distant.*

STANLEY: Out into the night, and then goodnight again! Whoops!

> (*He falls, not badly, but enough to see him to the ground.* JEAN *is out there in front of him.*)

MARCIA: Oh, Stanley . . .

STANLEY: (*Getting up*) The drinking of whisky . . . the drinking of gin . . .

> (*He smiles.* JEAN *has gone to the garden gate to see everyone away, and now turns.* MORGAN *has appeared in the doorway, seen through the shapes of the tottering* STANLEY *and the others.*)

MORGAN: It's been very pleasant. Would you mind if I came round again?

88

> (*They look at each other, across the distance.* STANLEY *suddenly addresses the night.*)

STANLEY: God, look at it! The night! The stars! Our lives!

> (MORGAN *suddenly smiles.*)

125. INT. JEAN'S HOUSE. NIGHT

The present. Night has come as JEAN *and* LANGDON *have sat together, the story unfolding. Now* LANGDON *gets up and, without looking at* JEAN, *he turns thoughtfully and walks to the far side of the room. There he turns, and then looking at her, walks quickly back across the room and takes her in his arms.*

LANGDON: There. There. Hold me tight.

> (*They embrace. Then he begins to kiss her, softly, kindly, all over her face. She kisses him. They rub their faces together, all the tension going out of them. They kiss again, their faces going down together side by side. All the memories go, as they embrace, their hands all over each other. Fade.*)

126. EXT. JEAN'S HOUSE. DAY

Next morning fades up. The house looks gentle, English, benevolent.

127. INT. SCHOOL CORRIDOR. DAY

JEAN *walks along the busy corridor, saying 'Good morning' distantly to various* PUPILS *as she passes.* ROGER *comes down the corridor. He looks down. She takes no notice. They pass. She goes on into the classroom.*

128. INT. CLASSROOM. DAY

JEAN *comes into her class. It is cheerful and noisy. It quietens down on her appearance.*

JEAN: Right everyone, good morning. First day of the week. Monday morning. Welcome. Windows, please. Gosh, a dirty blackboard already. (*Gets out a big book.*) Register. (*Looks round the class.*) Please, where's Suzie? (*There's silence.*) Does anyone know?

JOHN: (*The sly boy*) She's run away to London.

GIRL: With Alfred Egerton. In Science Fifth.

89

assorted oddballs, eccentrics, folk who still feel that school is worthwhile, I suggest we keep trying. All right, everyone?
(*She looks round smiling. They are pleased by this speech.*)
Good. Then let's work.

129. INT. LANGDON'S HOUSE. DAY
Langdon's room. LANGDON *is standing on one side of the room in his shirtsleeves, tie and suit trousers. His jacket lies across the unmade bed on the other side of the room. He is looking across at it. Then he moves across the room. His wallet and keys are lying on the dressing table. He opens the wallet. Inside, his CID card. He takes it out, looks at it, then tears it up into little pieces. They sprinkle down on the floor.*

130. EXT. LANGDON'S HOUSE. DAY
We go high above the housing estate as MIKE LANGDON *comes out of his front door in pullover and trousers and walks off down the road. A hundred little brick houses stretch away into the distance. The empty tarmac road glitters.*

131. INT. PUB. DAY
JEAN *sits alone in the pub. A wide shot, sitting alone in the smoke. Then, after a while,* STANLEY *appears.*
JEAN: How are you?
STANLEY: How are you?
(JEAN *smiles.*)
JEAN: I'm better. How's Marcia?
STANLEY: Oh, she's tremendous. Yes. The Charity Bridge Tournament takes all her time.
(*The* BAR GIRL *comes with a bottle of white wine. She puts it down. She is very young.* STANLEY *stares up at her, dazzled by her beauty. Then they watch her go, saying nothing.*)
When you're a boy, you think, oh, it's so easy. Always wipe the slate and move on. Then you find, with the years, you become the prisoner of dreams.
(JEAN *nods slightly.*)
JEAN: A girl ran away this morning.

STANLEY: Good luck to her.
JEAN: Yes. Good luck.
 (STANLEY *lifts his glass.*)
STANLEY: To all our escapes.
 (*They drink. We pull back. They are two among many. The
 low sound of conversation in the pub. They look around them.
 Fade.*)

her. It is very quiet suddenly. Their faces are very close together. We are way above them, and as they speak, we come closer slowly, creeping in. We can only just hear.

MORGAN: Listen, I know you're in trouble.

JEAN: What?

MORGAN: You're in trouble. Like me.

JEAN: I don't know what you mean.

MORGAN: Come on.

JEAN: No.

MORGAN: You're lonely.

JEAN: Yes, well, I'm lonely, I'm not in trouble.

MORGAN: Please don't argue with me. All that hope coming out of you. All that cheerful resolution. All that wonderful enlightenment. For what? For nothing. You know it's for nothing. Don't tell me that cheerfulness is real.

JEAN: Yes, of course.

MORGAN: You and I – we understand each other.

JEAN: What? No . . . what?

MORGAN: You fake. You fake all that cheerfulness.

JEAN: No, please. It's who I am.

MORGAN: Then why did you lead me up here?

JEAN: I didn't.

MORGAN: Liar! (*He twists her head and speaks into her ear.*) You know. You know where you're looking.

JEAN: I don't.

MORGAN: You've been here. Where I am.

(*She begins to struggle free of him, panicking, realizing the extent of his madness. At once he grabs at her sweater, but she wrenches herself free.*)

JEAN: I haven't. I'm sorry. I haven't been where you are. I have to change.

(*She has struggled up. There is blood running down her stocking.*)

MORGAN: No.

JEAN: Yes. *Please.*

(*She is about to move towards her room, when he grabs her arm. He looks at her with a sudden, terrifying ferocity.*)

MORGAN: *You will.*

124. EXT. JEAN'S HOUSE. NIGHT

Flashback. The house seen from a great distance. Lit windows in the night. The front door opens. The end of a dinner party. The sound of STANLEY, *very distant.*

STANLEY: Out into the night, and then goodnight again! Whoops!

   (*He falls, not badly, but enough to see him to the ground.* JEAN *is out there in front of him.*)

MARCIA: Oh, Stanley . . .

STANLEY: (*Getting up*) The drinking of whisky . . . the drinking of gin . . .

   (*He smiles.* JEAN *has gone to the garden gate to see everyone away, and now turns.* MORGAN *has appeared in the doorway, seen through the shapes of the tottering* STANLEY *and the others.*)

MORGAN: It's been very pleasant. Would you mind if I came round again?

88

(They look at each other, across the distance. STANLEY
suddenly addresses the night.)
STANLEY: God, look at it! The night! The stars! Our lives!
(MORGAN *suddenly smiles.*)

125. INT. JEAN'S HOUSE. NIGHT
The present. Night has come as JEAN *and* LANGDON *have sat
together, the story unfolding. Now* LANGDON *gets up and, without
looking at* JEAN, *he turns thoughtfully and walks to the far side of
the room. There he turns, and then looking at her, walks quickly
back across the room and takes her in his arms.*
LANGDON: There. There. Hold me tight.
*(They embrace. Then he begins to kiss her, softly, kindly, all
over her face. She kisses him. They rub their faces together, all
the tension going out of them. They kiss again, their faces going
down together side by side. All the memories go, as they
embrace, their hands all over each other. Fade.)*

126. EXT. JEAN'S HOUSE. DAY
Next morning fades up. The house looks gentle, English, benevolent.

127. INT. SCHOOL CORRIDOR. DAY
JEAN *walks along the busy corridor, saying 'Good morning' distantly
to various* PUPILS *as she passes.* ROGER *comes down the corridor.
He looks down. She takes no notice. They pass. She goes on into the
classroom.*

128. INT. CLASSROOM. DAY
JEAN *comes into her class. It is cheerful and noisy. It quietens down
on her appearance.*
JEAN: Right everyone, good morning. First day of the week.
Monday morning. Welcome. Windows, please. Gosh, a
dirty blackboard already. *(Gets out a big book.)* Register.
(Looks round the class.) Please, where's Suzie?
(There's silence.)
Does anyone know?
JOHN: *(The sly boy)* She's run away to London.
GIRL: With Alfred Egerton. In Science Fifth.

(*The* GIRL *giggles. Another* GIRL *thinks this the most hilarious thing.*)

JEAN: Has she been in touch with her parents?

GIRL: Oh yes, Miss.

JEAN: Good.

BOY: (*From the back of the class*) She said she couldn't see the point of school.

JEAN: (*Serious, quiet*) No, well, sometimes I have that problem. (*Looks round the class.*) Anyone else? Anyone else want to go?

(*There is a silence, profound, as if recognizing her seriousness.*) You are free. You are free to go if you wish.

(*The whole class seen in wide shot, quite still. Then* JEAN *speaks very quietly.*)

Right then, for those of us still remaining – us maniacs,